"Excuse me," I said, "but could we borrow your ketchup for a minute? We don't have any at our table and we can't seem to attract the waitress's attention."

The Mack Look-alike smiled and said, "I thought you'd never ask."

He was friendly. I knew he would be. After all, he'd been nice to Heidi. Could this be the start of something? Why had I done this?

Mack Look-alike handed the container of ketchup to me. "I'll bring it right back," I said.

"We'll be here," he said.

I went back to my table with the ketchup. I looked back at the next table. The three people had their heads together and were talking. I realized that they might have been talking about me. Had they noticed that there were at least ten other ketchup containers on unoccupied tables?

MARJORIE SHARMAT is the author of nearly a hundred books, including *How to Meet a Gorgeous Guy, How to Meet a Gorgeous Girl, How to Have a Gorgeous Wedding, I Saw Him First, He Noticed I'm Alive . . . and Other Hopeful Signs,* and *Two Guys Noticed Me . . . and Other Miracles,* all available in Dell Laurel-Leaf editions. She lives with her husband in Tucson, Arizona.

ALSO AVAILABLE IN LAUREL-LEAF BOOKS:

Vacation Fever!

MARJORIE SHARMAT

LAUREL-LEAF BOOKS

Published by
Dell Publishing
a division of
Bantam Doubleday Dell Publishing Group, Inc.
666 Fifth Avenue
New York, New York 10103

This work was first published in the U.S. in 1984 by Pacer
Books, a member of The Putnam & Grosset Group, under
the pseudonym Wendy Andrews.

ISBN: 0-440-20677-4

RL: 5.3

Published by arrangement with the author

Printed in the United States of America

July 1990

10 9 8 7 6 5 4 3 2 1

RAD

for a certain March 11th
when I caught vacation fever
in Miami Beach, Florida

Vacation Fever!

1

"I can't believe they're making me go with them!"

Everyone in the pizza parlor turned and stared at me. I hadn't intended to tell everybody my personal business, but when I get mad, my voice rises. My friend Kristi claims that a weird glint also appears in my eyes.

"Shh," she said. "You don't want everyone to hear you, do you?"

"I don't care, I'm so furious. I've only got a few weeks left of my summer vacation, and I don't want to spend them with my aunt and uncle and other scenic attractions in Dallas, Texas."

"Your aunt and uncle are scenic attractions?"

"You know what I mean. I worked hard this summer, right? I'm starting senior year this September, right? So these three weeks are supposed to be *mine*, right?"

"And Mack Hampton's. And Phil Reeves'. And Cal Gillman's."

"Okay, so finally I've been going out a lot. I'm having a very successful social summer. And now I'm being driven about a thousand miles away from the scene of my success."

"Phoenix will be here when you get back. Aren't you eating your mushrooms?" Kristi was eyeing my pizza.

"I'm not hungry. My sister and brother don't want to go either. Does your family ever vote? I mean, there are two parents and three kids, so my parents are outnumbered three to two."

"Ha! You're out*aged*. That's the only thing that counts. Parents have the power, haven't you noticed?"

"Yeah, the power to squeeze me into the backseat of a car between a fifteen-year-old car freak and an eleven-year-old TV freak while all my friends are back here."

"Just tell your parents that you don't want to go, Mia."

"I did. But they say it's our last chance to take a trip as a family. They say I'll be leaving the nest next fall. Mia Fisher, the nest-leaver. I'm committing a capital crime."

"How about Ted and Heidi? Aren't they kicking and screaming?"

"You bet. Ted just got his learner's permit and now he wants his own car. I think he's trying to impress Emily Remmick. He says that this trip will interrupt

10

his goals. His goals, isn't that a laugh? And Heidi, she just hangs around and watches TV all day. You can't do that in a car. At least not in the car we own. She's so lazy. When I was eleven, I must have done something besides watch TV all summer. Didn't I?"

"I forget. But it sounds like she'd enjoy a break."

"A break? She says the trip is a yucky idea, and that relatives are yucky and they'll kiss her too much and ask her stupid questions. Also, she manages to get carsick at inconvenient times. She has a highly developed talent for getting revenge."

"This doesn't seem like a great way to start a trip," said Kristi. "Still, maybe you'll all get lucky and get vacation fever."

"Vacation fever?"

"Sure. Almost everybody who goes on vacation gets it. It's a kind of excitement that takes over when you go to new places and meet new people. It's the possibility of romance and the kind of adventure you'd never find at home. Your whole family will probably get it in one form or another."

"It's a communicable disease?"

"Don't joke, Mia. You'll be meeting new guys. You can be adventurous, you can wear purple makeup, you can be a little crazy. You can pretend to be anyone you want to be. You have nothing to lose. I wish I were going."

"You do?"

"Yeah. This trip could be something wonderful you can look back on and dream about when blah Febru-

11

ary rolls around. Go for it. Let vacation fever penetrate every pore in your body."

"I'll try to catch it. No promises."

"Let me know everything that happens," said Kristi. "Send me plenty of postcards."

"Put my private life on postcards for the whole world to see? No way."

"You want me to wait until you *come back?* Are you crazy?"

Poor Kristi. I could see that she wanted to take that vacation right along with me.

"Okay, okay," I said. "I'll do the best I can."

"Fair enough," said Kristi. "Can I have all your mushrooms?"

Dear Kristi,
We're off! And you'd better be right about V.F. (Vacation Fever, of course).

Love,
Mia

2

I was squeezed in the middle of the backseat. I always am when Ted, Heidi, and I go anywhere in the car with our parents. How it had started and why it has continued, I don't know. My brother on the left is thin. My sister on the right is overweight. She constantly eats while she watches TV, which means she constantly eats. My mother and father were sitting in front innocently, as if they weren't transporting three captives in the rear.

"We have a lovely day to start our trip," my mother said. "Did you pack the hangers, Mia?"

"Oh, Mom. Motels have hangers. Break the hanger habit. We could hardly close the car trunk as it is because we packed so much stuff."

"It's not a habit. It's a precaution. You don't know whose clothes were on those metal hangers. No one ever thinks to wash them."

"Stop worrying, Mom."

My mother is a full-time worrier. When she's home, she has a stable, fairly consistent number of things to worry about. On the road, the possibilities stretched without limitation. I leaned back. How did I get stuck in this situation? I wasn't a kid anymore. Why should I get dragged along as part of a family unit? I'd definitely outgrown this. The more I thought about Kristi's vacation fever, the more I wanted it. A new guy. A new Mia. Adventure. But how could I possibly find it when I was attached to four other people?

"Did you pack the Thermos of coffee and the sandwiches, Hugh?" This question was directed at my father.

"Sure. And if I hadn't, I suspect we could find a coffee and sandwich place within the next thousand miles." My father smiled.

"This trip is costing us enough," said my mother. "Little economies can make the difference."

"If you left Heidi and Mia and me at home, you could have saved a bundle," said Ted. He nudged me. "Pass it on," he said.

"Let's not talk. Let's just enjoy the scenery," said my mother.

"But we're only twenty or thirty miles from home," Heidi said. "I've seen this scenery a million times."

I was silent. Each mile was taking me farther away from my friends. From Kristi. From Phil. From Mack. From Cal. From all the fun.

"I'm hungry," said Heidi.

"But you just had a snack twenty-five miles ago," my mother said.

14

"I'm hungry. I'd be watching *Space Spooks* and eating right now if I hadn't come on this trip."

My mother fished in a bag at her feet. She pulled out a sandwich wrapped in foil and gave it to Heidi. "Here. Peanut butter and jelly."

"Yuck. This is home food," said Heidi. "Why do I have to eat home food when I'm not home? I want to eat in a restaurant. I want to sit at a table and have somebody wait on me."

Heidi fingered the sandwich. "The sun got to it through the window."

"Pretend it's toasted," said my mother.

"We'll eat in a restaurant later," said my father. "When I need a break from this driving."

"I'll help you drive," said Ted.

"No you won't. This is no place for you to practice. This trip requires a very experienced driver."

"You'll change your mind when you get desperate."

"No, I won't. You and Mia won't be driving on this trip."

"I don't care," I said.

"I wish I had learned to drive," said my mother. "But there are so many cars on the road."

"That's the general idea, Mom," Ted said.

"You didn't put enough jelly in this sandwich," Heidi said.

"Hugh, did you have the air-conditioning checked thoroughly? I'm worried about all the driving we'll be doing through the desert."

"This is a desert sandwich," said Heidi. "All dry."

I let the conversation drift over my head. I was

15

thinking about Phil and Cal and Mack. Especially
Mack Hampton. He was probably my favorite. I had
never been so popular, and now I was going away and
they'd forget me. Even if I did send postcards. You
can't date a picture of the moon rising over oil pumps
and cattle.

"You're making a face, Mia," my mother said. My
mother spends half the time looking at the backseat
when we're in the car.

"If you don't stop, your face will stay that way forever and the boys won't like you anymore," said
Heidi.

"Oh, be quiet. Boys like me for my intelligence."

"Haw, haw, haw," Ted said. "What intelligence?
Show me. Can I touch it?"

"I want harmony back there," said my mother. "So
your father can concentrate on his driving. Please
keep in mind that this is a special trip, that we'll
probably never be together in quite the same way
again."

"Is that a promise?" asked Ted.

I closed my eyes. It was too early in the trip to take
a nap, and there wasn't any room anyway. But at
least I could withdraw from the conversation. My
withdrawal was complete. I dozed off. I woke when
the car came to a stop.

"You slept for well over an hour," my father said.
"We're stopping for a bite to eat and some leg stretch-
ing. This looks like a decent place. A couple of trucks
in the parking lot."

"It's a myth," said Ted, "that truckers know the

16

best places to eat. I'm studying up on vehicles and one of my books stated that."

"Trucks or not, we're already here," said my mother. She opened the car door and got out. She stretched. "That feels good. Come on, everybody, stretch."

The rest of us got out of the car. "I'll stretch later," said Heidi. "It looks dumb for all of us to stretch at once. What if someone is looking?"

"Nobody's looking," said my mother.

"The people in the next car are looking," said Ted.

I glanced at the next car. Three persons were sitting in it, watching us. One of them looked like Mack. It couldn't be Mack, unless he were visiting Tucson. We weren't far from there. Maybe he was already on the lookout for new girls.

"Let's just stare them down," Heidi said. She turned and stared at the three people.

They got out of their car and walked toward the restaurant. They were a middle-aged couple and what appeared to be their teenage son. Or he could have been twenty. Whatever his age was, he did a nice job with it. He did look like Mack. I felt part of myself wake up, the first time since the trip had started. I wondered what *I* looked like. My hair must be a wreck after dozing on it. But so what? The guy was just a person going into a restaurant whom I'd never see again. And besides, I was with my *family*. That would kill any chance of romance. Still, Kristi *believed* in vacation fever. "You'll be meeting new

17

guys," she had said. "You can be adventurous. You can pretend to be anyone you want to be."

"Let's go, gang," said my father. We started to walk through the parking lot.

"This restaurant isn't part of a chain," Heidi said. "I bet they don't even advertise on TV or have their own jingle or anything. How come we're eating in a restaurant that isn't on TV?"

Heidi rushed ahead to size up the restaurant. She tripped on the curb.

"Hey!" said the Mack Look-alike. He caught Heidi as she was about to fall. "You're not that hungry, are you?"

"Not for *their* food," Heidi said. "This is an anonymous restaurant. They don't advertise on TV."

"Maybe anonymous food tastes good," said the guy. "Are you okay? Did you hurt yourself?"

"No, you caught me just in time. Thanks."

"Anytime. Just be careful. You don't want to ruin your vacation, do you?"

"Maybe. We're going to Dallas."

"Dallas? That's great. I once . . ."

Mack Look-alike didn't have a chance to finish his sentence. The woman who was probably his mother called, "Dear, we're waiting."

"Excuse me," he said to Heidi. "Enjoy your meal."

He walked off. My parents, Ted, and I had come up behind him. Part of me was feeling aggressive. I wanted to introduce myself, maybe thank him, but it was too late.

"I just met an interesting older person," Heidi said. "Isn't that what you're supposed to do on vacation?"

"As long as they're nice," said my mother.

"He was nice," Heidi said.

I thought so, too. I wished *I* had met him.

Inside the restaurant we took a table beside the table where the three people had sat down. It just seemed to happen that way. I faced the guy who looked like Mack. Now I wished I were dressed better. I had put on my worst shorts and a faded shirt in honor of this trip I didn't want to make. My sandals were scuffed. My mother was examining and wiping off the silverware as the waitress approached us and gave high praise to the special of the day.

"Do you have a children's special?" my mother asked.

"Mom!" said Heidi. "No!" Heidi turned to speak to the waitress. "We have no children here. I'll have a hamburger with a side order of fries and a lime soda."

"I'll have the same," I said. I didn't want to spend time studying the menu when I could study the Mack Look-alike at the next table. Where did he come from and where was he going? I wondered.

My father unfolded a map while we waited for the food to come. My dad is a high-school teacher, but he doesn't do things like a teacher. At least not when he's traveling. He didn't have a plan for each day, he didn't make reservations in advance to ensure that we'd have a place to stay every night. He was casual about everything. Since Mom was willing to worry

19

about everything, there wasn't any point in the two of them doing the same thing. His casualness and her worrying were actually in harmony. My mother didn't want to make reservations at any place until she had seen it with her own eyes. They had decided they would allow about a week to get to my aunt's and uncle's place. They could have made it in three or four days, but this gave them a chance to stay an extra night or two if they found any places that they liked.

My mother's a teacher, too. They both teach at the same high school. Dad's classes are informal. Mom's classes are structured. The students in Mom's classes get a better education, but Dad's students think that learning is fun. I suspect that someday one of them will be fired when the high school decides which type of education is superior.

Everyone ordered hamburgers, which made Heidi feel like a leader. The waitress plopped the food on our table and left.

"Hey, where's the ketchup?" Ted asked of the empty space where the waitress had stood seconds before.

"Get her back, Hugh," my mother said.

"She's abandoned us," my father said. "A new group just came in to be served."

Ted nudged me. "You're sitting on the end, Mia. Go get the ketchup."

I was about to tell him to stop giving me orders. But then I had an idea: this could be a perfect chance for a vacation adventure. I stood up and walked over

20

to the next table where the three people were sitting. On the table was a container of ketchup. Of course there were also containers of ketchup on most of the unoccupied tables in the room.

"Excuse me," I said, "but could we borrow your ketchup for a minute? We don't have any at our table and we can't seem to attract the waitress's attention."

The Mack Look-alike smiled and said, "I thought you'd never ask."

He was friendly. I knew he would be. After all, he'd been nice to Heidi. Could this be the start of something? Why had I done this?

Mack Look-alike handed the container of ketchup to me. "I'll bring it right back," I said.

"We'll be here," he said.

I went back to my table with the ketchup. I looked back at the next table. The three people had their heads together and were talking. I realized that they might have been talking about me. Had they noticed that there were at least ten other ketchup containers on unoccupied tables?

"Back in business?" Ted said. "Can't you forget boys for five minutes? There's ketchup all over this room. Why didn't you ask to borrow his handkerchief? I don't see any handkerchiefs."

"Oh, be quiet, Ted. I've seen you in operation with Emily Remmick. So just clam up unless you want me to discuss the Cadillac dealership you're planning to own in the very near future. That *is* what you told Emily, isn't it?"

"Dear," my mother said to me, "it was a bit obvious to ask for *their* ketchup when all the other ketchup containers were staring us in the face."

"They were happy to lend theirs," I said. "Now could I please enjoy my hamburger?"

"She's right, Gwen," my father said to my mother. "Let's all relax."

I ate my hamburger with my eyes fixed on the next table. Mack Look-alike was at an angle to me, but he turned and smiled. Was he smiling at me or at Heidi? I smiled back, and since I didn't know exactly what else to do, I pointed to the container as if to say that his ketchup was wonderful. That was pretty stupid but I couldn't help myself. I finished my hamburger quickly. I decided to return the ketchup before he left. If I didn't do something, nothing would happen on this vacation.

I turned to my family. "All through with the ketchup?" I squirted more ketchup out of the plastic container onto my plate. It made a little round red mountain. "If you need more, just use this." I got up and took the container back to the next table before they could say anything. The three people were getting ready to leave.

"Thanks so much," I said as I put the container on the table. "What are hamburgers and fries without ketchup?"

The couple looked at me in an uneasy way. Mack Look-alike was holding the check. I felt like an intruder, but I wanted to prolong my stay. "On a trip?" I asked the woman.

"Yes," she said. She smiled weakly. She was going to be polite, but she was not offering more than that.

Mack Look-alike looked up from the check. "We're from San Diego," he said. Into my head there immediately flashed memories of all the airline ads I had seen showing how quickly one can travel between San Diego and Phoenix. Mack Look-alike didn't live that far from me. "We're touring Arizona and New Mexico. We've about wrapped up Arizona and we're on our way to New Mexico."

"So am I," I said. "Looks like we're going in the same direction."

"I thought you were heading for Dallas?"

"Dallas. I mean, I have to get to Dallas sometime, but right now I'm heading for New Mexico. Wait, how did you know that?"

"Your little sister told me. That *is* your little sister?"

The woman's smile was still on her face. The man was taking some bills from his wallet.

"Yes, she is." I hesitated. "Uh, we haven't reserved a motel for tonight. You wouldn't know of a good place to stay, would you? Clean and safe?"

"Indeed we do," said the woman. "We're staying with relatives." She nudged the man as if to say, Let's get out of here.

Mack Look-alike grinned at me. "Maybe we'll meet along the way."

"Yeah, maybe."

I walked back to my table.

"You met my friend," said Heidi.

"Your friend," Ted said. "All he did was help you in the parking lot."

"I know a friend when I see one," said Heidi. "And he thinks of me that way, too. He's the biggest friend I've got."

"If he's your friend, what's his name?" asked Ted.

"Names aren't important," Heidi said. "So, Mia, what did he say to you?"

"Yes, what was that all about?" asked my mother. "We couldn't hear the conversation from here."

"It was nothing." I watched the three people leave the restaurant. I felt so drained. It was the same feeling I had when I began the trip.

Back on the road, my mother decided we should sing some songs. "Mom, this isn't a school field trip," I said. "None of us wants to sing." One night a few years ago we had turned off the TV set and sat around the piano and sang songs while my mother played the piano. My mother never forgot this. She thought we were the new Trapp Family Singers and a collective career had been launched. The night was more of an aberration than a beginning. Ted, especially, couldn't stand feeling that wholesome.

"Can you get a rock station on the radio?" he was asking my mother now.

"No radio," said my mother. "It will confuse your father while he's driving. Just watch the scenery."

"The scenery's the same as before," said Heidi. "How can we drive so far without the scenery changing?"

24

"I guess it's just a miracle," said Ted, and he took a paperback car manual out of his pocket.

"Don't read in the car," said my mother. "You'll get carsick. When you were younger, you always threw up on car trips. It could come back."

"Aw, Ma, this is the first fun I've had."

"Very well." My mother gazed out the window. "America the beautiful," she said.

"America the hot," said Heidi. "Are you sure the air-conditioning is working?"

"It's working," said my father.

"This might be your last opportunity to see a mesquite tree on this trip. Look how lovely they are," said my mother. "Are there mesquite trees in New Mexico, Hugh?"

"Lovely?" said Ted. "Is that another word for ugly?"

I looked out the window because there was nothing else to do. Besides, it was better to concentrate on bad scenery than on the fool I had made of myself in the restaurant. Why should I dwell on it anyway? I'd never see any of them again. He *was* cute, and he was really friendly. But those other two were aloof. I guess they're his parents. Could he be stuck on a trip like me? Maybe I was the highlight of his trip. How sad, I thought, I'll never know. I was ready for romance and all I had were mesquite trees.

"Are we there yet?" asked Heidi.

"We've hardly begun," said my mother.

Three hours later, at Heidi's request, my mother

25

passed out more sandwiches. "Our provisions are all gone now," she said. "No more food." She was hoping to make a little adventure out of our used-up supplies.

"I'm crying," said Ted. "Our wagon train is sure to die."

Everyone was quiet for the next couple of hours, as if by signal. We were getting tired. Ted whipped out the handheld video game he had brought along. In the game he had to track some cats in a cat track meet. I got dizzy when I looked at it.

My mother said, "It's time to find a place to stay for the night."

"Let's camp out," said Ted. "It's cheap and it'll be fun. C'mon."

"Nothing doing," I said. "Fun for you and agony for me. I hate camping out."

"You never camp out, so how do you know?"

"I know."

"I see a vacancy sign up ahead," said my father. He turned toward my mother. "Want to give it a try?"

"Looks a little run-down," my mother said. "The M is out in the motel sign. That's a bad sign."

"Bad sign? Is that a pun? Which way do you mean it?" Ted asked.

I watched wearily as my father approached and then drove past motel after motel that did not meet my mother's standards. Once they almost agreed on a motel before they noticed that the *No* was lit up just in front of *VACANCY* on the sign. It was getting dark.

"Please, Dad, Mom," I said, "let's just check into the next place. Even if it's a fleabag."

My mother shook her head yes.

"I can drive if Dad's tired," said Ted. "And we can keep on looking, Mom."

"Don't try to make a deal, Ted," said Heidi. "I'm tired."

"There's a place just ahead," said my father. "This is it."

My mother peered out the window. "It looks very nice. Too nice. Can we afford it?"

Heidi groaned. "I don't believe this."

My father turned into the motel parking lot. "This is it," he said. "We agreed." He parked near a sign that said OFFICE. "Wait here and I'll check in."

At last! I thought as I looked at the motel. It was attractive, with hedges and flower arrangements and what appeared in the dark to be a smooth expanse of lawn. There was probably a swimming pool in back. The sign had said pool and TV. Not that I cared. I was tired and cramped. Being with the family was getting to be too much. I was learning fast that it's possible to love people but not want to be with them all the time. Especially in a middle-of-the-sandwich position in a backseat.

Suddenly I sat straight up. Something had caught my attention. There were three people walking into the motel office just ahead of my father. They looked familiar, but from the back I couldn't be sure. Then one of them laughed. Under the light I saw Mack Look-alike. The three of them were checking into the motel.

Some relatives, I thought.

27

Dear Kristi,
   Never borrow ketchup from a stranger.

               Your frustrated pal,
                    Mia

3

"I'll go see what's keeping Dad," I said. I started out of the car before my mother could object. My father had been in the motel office for probably less than three minutes.

"Hey, you're going in the wrong direction, Mia."

My father was coming back to the car. He was holding keys. "We're all set."

"I'll be right back," I said, and started to pass my father. "Oh, forget it. I'm coming."

I went back to the car. My father drove it up to Room 116. The motel was two stories. Our accommodations were on the ground floor.

"It's all they had for adjoining rooms," my father explained to my mother. "I know you don't like the ground floor."

"It's more vulnerable to break-ins and you can hear the footsteps of the people above you," my mother said. "Never mind. We're lucky to get this. How much did they charge?"

"You don't want to know."

Now my mother really wanted to know. But Ted interrupted. "Want me to unload the trunk, Dad?"

"Now you're getting into the spirit of the trip, son."

"No, all I'm doing is offering to unload the trunk."

"We'll just take in what we need for the night," said my father. "The rest will be safe out here, but we'll have to make sure the trunk is locked securely."

"We can all share the toothpaste and shampoo and that sort of thing," said my mother. "All we need are our nightclothes."

"I'll sleep in my underwear," said Ted.

"I won't," said Heidi. "Where's my stuff?"

"I packed it," said my mother. "Mia, do you know where your things are?"

"The gray suitcase has everything I need," I said.

"Then we're all set," said my father.

"Can I have my own room?" asked Heidi.

"Of course not, dear," said my mother. "Your father and Ted will sleep in one room, and you, Mia, and I will sleep in the other."

"Is there a cot? Do I get the cot? When Courtney takes trips with her family she always has to sleep on the cot. She says it's gross."

"I'll take the cot," I said. Heidi was the youngest. She needed status badly. I knew she would have been assigned the cot, just the way she got hand-me-down clothes, just the way her opinions were valued the

29

least. Nobody intended to slight her. It just worked out that way. I didn't mind taking the cot. I minded taking the room! No privacy.

Heidi was aware of my sacrificial act. She smiled and said, "Thanks, Mia."

And I said, "Okay, you owe me one." Maybe the guy liked her and not me. Maybe Heidi could help me find out about him.

The rooms were identical and joined by a common door. "They're kind of pleasant, actually," said my mother. She pressed mattresses. "Firm."

I put my suitcase on a bed and started to unpack. My mother looked shocked. "You packed your ratty clothes," she said.

"Ratty? Where did you get a word like that?" I asked.

"From you, of course. I remember distinctly that you described these clothes as ratty. I know you own better. Don't you want to look nice for your aunt and uncle?"

"Not especially. Don't get me wrong. They're okay, I like them as relatives, but why couldn't they have visited us?"

"We've been over this a dozen times. This trip gives us a chance to see some of the country *and* your aunt and uncle. We're fortunate that they've only recently moved to Dallas and they're still willing to have us as guests."

Willing to have us as guests? My mother and her sister, my aunt, are so close that my mother is more of a shadow of my aunt than a guest. Or maybe my aunt is a shadow of my mother. They're always on the phone long-distance. I think my father agreed to this trip so he could save on phone bills.

"Isn't that the dress with the split seams?" My mother was still analyzing my wardrobe.

"Yeah."

"Did you repair it?"

"No. I read somewhere in a hints column that you should take along your worst clothes on a trip and throw out each item after it's worn."

My mother frowned.

"Aren't we going to eat supper?" asked Heidi. "I'm hungry."

"There's a coffee shop here," said my mother. "As soon as we settle in, we'll go eat."

"I'll meet you there," I said, and I left before anyone could ask questions. It seemed logical to me that Mack Look-alike could be at the coffee shop. I'd love to see the look on the faces of the Ketchup Trio when they see me and know I've seen them. Let that lady squirm.

I felt nervous as I walked into the coffee shop. I looked around. I didn't recognize anybody. I caught a glimpse of myself in a small mirror near the entrance. I looked grubby. Maybe it was for the best that Mack Look-alike wasn't there.

I slid into a booth and waited for my family. What a drag this trip was. Sitting in a booth in a coffee shop by myself when I could be out with Mack and be a real, accepted, noticed, admired person. I picked up the menu and studied it.

Someone slid into the other side of the booth. "Hello Ketchup Girl."

It was Mack Look-alike!

"Hello," I said. Was I mad at him or just at the woman who had been with him? I couldn't remember. As I looked at his chiseled face and amazing blue eyes, I decided I didn't believe in guilt by association. He was better-looking than Mack. And different, really. He wasn't responsible for the mean lady who was probably his mother.

"Are you alone?" he asked.

"Temporarily."

"Where's your family?"

"They're changing. I'm not really *with* them. They're taking this trip to visit relatives, and I'm just kind of keeping them company. How about you?"

"I'm with my parents too."

"Do you have to travel with them? I mean, isn't it a drag traveling with your parents?"

"No, they're doing me the favor. I'm entering college in the fall and this is my last leisurely first-class vacation with no responsibilities."

"What an interesting way to look at it."

"Is there another way?"

"Well, didn't you leave friends behind in San Diego? Don't you miss them?"

"They won't run away."

"I guess not."

It didn't sound to me as if he left anyone *really* interesting in San Diego. Like a girl.

32

He was gazing at me with his blue eyes. Mack vanished. Why had I thought he looked like Mack?

He said, "I can't get over the coincidence of our landing up in the same motel."

"Neither can I. How did you pick it?"

"My mother picked it. She says it's the best in the area. She made reservations way in advance. She's a fussy person."

"Then it really isn't a coincidence," I said. "My mother's fussy, too. We passed place after place that didn't live up to her standards. They were probably the same places your mother decided against when she made reservations for here. By the time we got here, though, we would have stayed if it were a dump."

He stood up suddenly. Was this the end? Hello and good-bye? "I see my folks," he said. "I have to run. Maybe we can meet later and we'll talk some more? How about eleven tonight in front of the motel office?"

"I'd love to, but I don't know. It might be . . . Never mind, that's fine. Eleven. I'll be there."

"Great. My name's Neal Guest, by the way. And say hi to your sweet sister."

"I will," I said. "And I'm Mia Fisher."

Neal joined his mother and father at a table. His mother kept glancing over toward me. I pretended not to notice. She probably thought I spirited him over here. I knew her type. She belonged to the generation where the guy always made the first move. I could see her waiting by her telephone for days, weeks, months. She's sitting there, reading a book on good manners. Her hands are busy knitting. She knits and knits. She produces enough sweaters and scarves to clothe every living being in the city of San Diego or wherever she grew up, and still she won't pick up the phone and make the first move.

I decided to stare back at her. Her clothes were ridiculous. Of course mine were ratty, but hers were created for a much younger person. She seemed so proper, she should have been wearing something ancient and Victorian. Not from the teen scene. She probably had no good qualities except having her son, Neal Guest. It was a nice name. That's what I thought until a sickening feeling spread over me. *Guest.* He was a motel guest. Did he just make it up? It was easy enough to come up with a phony name like that under these circumstances. If he made it up, it was more devious than Jones or Smith because it was a kind of joke, in addition, and it was being played on me. Still, his mother looked like a Mrs. Guest. No first name, just Mrs. Guest. It suited her. I made myself believe he was Neal Guest.

All through dinner with my family I thought about Neal. How was I going to meet him at eleven? Kristi would know how. Here it was, Kristi. This was *it!* A fantastic guy on a vacation, an actual date, and my only problem was that I was imprisoned by my family. My mother would have a fit. Meeting a guy I hardly knew outside a motel office at eleven o'clock at night probably couldn't be topped as an unacceptable proposition to put to her.

I'll just sneak out. She'll go to bed early because of Heidi, and that will take care of that!

"Is everybody happy with this motel?" My father was speaking.

"Definitely," I said.

"We were fortunate to find it," said my mother. "So far this trip has gone smoothly. I hope you children are having a good time."

"I will if I can drive tomorrow," Ted said. "Dad, do you know what happens when you start up a cold engine? Engine parts rub against each other, there's very little or no lubrication, fuel is consumed like crazy. It's a traumatic time for your car."

"Really?" said my father. He looked amused. "And what do you propose to do about it?"

"I could start the car for you. I'm knowledgeable. I could drive a bit, too. You could rest. Fatigue is cumulative. Tomorrow you'll be more tired than you were today."

"Don't count on it," said my father. He was still amused.

"We'll be stopping somewhere for more than one night," my mother said. "We may stay as many as three nights in one place if we find a good spot. Your father will have a chance to rest up then."

"You do look tired, Dad," Heidi said.

I noticed that both of my parents looked tired. Neal was obviously a good influence on me. After I thought about his attitude toward his vacation, I began to appreciate how much planning and effort my parents had made. They had one purpose: they wanted the family to have a happy vacation. Maybe I could try to be a bit more cooperative. In prison sometimes they let you out early for good behavior. Yes, I was sure my new frame of mind had something to do with meeting Neal. If only I could have more to do with him . . . Tonight could be a start.

It was nine o'clock when we got back to our rooms. My father and Ted said good night and went to their room. Now if only my mother and Heidi would get undressed and go to sleep . . . Heidi turned on the television set. She could watch for hours!

"There's nothing on tonight, Heidi," I said.

"Are you kidding? This is the best night of the week."

"When are we going to bed? If we're going to be up a long time, maybe I'll take a walk later on."

"Outside? In a strange place? Absolutely not," said my mother.

"You worry too much," I said. "You treat me like a baby."

My mother wanted me to be safe from everything. It was an impossible goal. She was just one person and she imagined all kinds of dangers out there. She meant well, but she was carrying too heavy a load in her head.

Heidi insisted on watching TV. She was starved for it. She hadn't seen a program in twenty-four hours.

She changed into her pajamas, then she turned on the set and snuggled under the bedcovers.

I tried to figure out how I could stay dressed. It looks suspicious to go to bed with your clothes on. Still, Ted was going to sleep in his underwear.

"I'm not going to fish around in my suitcase anymore," I said. "I'll just sleep in what I'm wearing, and tomorrow I'll shower and change."

My mother didn't put up a fuss. She was too tired to make an issue over clothes. She sat brushing her short blond-gray hair, which she did every night even though I had warned her that too much brushing can harm hair.

My mother's ideas of what was harmful and what was not are entrenched, and anything that sprung from her childhood traditions and habits could not possibly be harmful. In appearance my mother also has not completely broken away from her childhood. She is unusual-looking. She has a short, chubby body and she resembles a mature doll. Her round, clear doll's face is rosy-cheeked and big-eyed, with lots of fringy eyelashes. She doesn't look like a teacher, but rather like something that has unexpectedly come to life from a shelf. I am used to the way she looks, but sometimes she startles strangers because she looks ten years old and forty years old at the same time. I love her, but I am secretly glad I look more like my father. My father is crazy about my mother. He doesn't look like a teacher either. Not to brag, but he's really attractive for a father. He's strong and muscular and most people would guess that he does something physical and sweaty for a living. Women are attracted to him, but I don't think he knows it.

Heidi fell asleep. My mother turned off the TV set and quietly signaled to me that we should go to bed, too. I looked at my watch. It was twenty minutes to ten. My mother turned out the lights. I turned down the sheets and blankets on the cot and climbed in. It was uncomfortable. I felt justified in leaving it. But I had an hour and twenty minutes to wait. My mother would be asleep long before then. There would be no trouble in slipping out. But what about getting back in? I hadn't thought this thing through. Where was the key to the room? The door would probably lock when I went out. I could fiddle with it and see if I could leave it unlocked. But that could wake my mother and Heidi. Besides, I couldn't see what I was doing. I didn't know anything about locks. I could leave the door ajar. No! Bugs, lights, intruders, who knows what would come in.

I was trapped in the room. Neal would wait for me by the office and I wouldn't show up. It would be like one of those classic love stories where lovers keep missing each other. Except this was my first chance and maybe my last.

I tried to fall asleep. I must have tried for an hour. I got up. I slipped into my sandals. Now what? I couldn't see anything. The room was dark except for a slit of light where the drapes didn't meet. My mother had forgotten to plug in her night-light. She always travels with a night-light.

I groped my way to the door. Slowly I turned the knob.

"Stop," said my mother. "Where are you going, Mia?"

"I thought you were sleeping, Mom."

"I'm not. What are you doing?"

"I couldn't sleep, so I decided to go for a little walk. I'll be back soon. Don't worry about me."

"I won't. But I can't sleep either. I'm going, too."

"You can't!"

"What do you mean I can't? I won't have you prowling around out there in the dark all by yourself."

I heard my mother get out of bed. She really meant it. She was going to escort me. I moved away from the door. "I changed my mind," I said. "I guess I'm too tired to walk."

"It will probably help you fall asleep. Come. We'll go together."

"Mom, you're not dressed."

"I've got a robe. It's good enough. We won't go far."

I peered out into the night. The outside of the motel was fairly well lit. I looked toward the office. Standing under a light was Neal. I felt so excited. He remembered. He was waiting. But I just couldn't go out there in the night with my mother.

"Mom, I'm not going." I said it very firmly. Maybe it would deter her from going. "Let's try to go to sleep."

"No, Mia, I really feel like a walk. I'll be back soon."

My mother put on her robe, stuck her feet into her

39

slippers, and shuffled out. She walked toward the motel office. I saw her stop and talk to Neal. Was she checking up on me? What would she say to him? I hoped Neal didn't think I *sent* my mother.

But there she was, sharing a romantic moon with my date. Just the two of them, far from home, together. It was ridiculous. *I* was supposed to be out there with Neal! Kristi would crack up if she knew what happened. But I could never tell her.

I slammed the door in disgust. I forgot about Heidi, but she didn't wake up. I climbed back into my cot. I shut my eyes and tried to forget the whole thing. I must have dozed off because a banging on the door woke me. Someone was trying to get into the room. It was my mother. I got up to let her in, and it dawned on me that she had totally carried out *my* plan. She had gone outside and met and talked with Neal. Then she got locked out of the room just as I had predicted I would. I could scream!

I let my mother in from her big night out on the town. I was anxious to know what she and Neal had talked about, but I didn't want to ask. I guess she didn't want to tell. "There are crickets everywhere out there," she said, and she went to bed.

Would I have another chance with Neal? I shut my eyes again. I was afraid I'd have a bad dream or even a nightmare: Neal, bearing gifts, would knock on my door, pat my head fondly, and hand me a nicely wrapped rattle, playpen, and stuffed panda.

Dear Kristi,
Two questions. Why did you allow me to pack ratty clothes?? Did you ever notice that my mother has ESP??
Yours in humiliation,
Mia

4

My father went out the next morning and bought two packages of sweet rolls, a container of orange juice, and a container of milk from a supermarket. My mother had brought along the family's famous old aluminum coffeepot. It went everywhere our family went. She filled it with water and plugged its cord into an outlet. Then she opened a jar of instant coffee that she had packed. *"Voilà* our breakfast," she said as she handed out the Styrofoam cups she had also packed and the little packets of sugar she had spirited out of the motel coffee shop the night before.

Ted groaned. "You and your economies. What did I tell you about the wear and tear of short trips on a car? Driving the car to the supermarket to buy breakfast? It would have been cheaper to eat in the coffee shop."

And better, too, I thought. My morning plan to look for Neal in the coffee shop died.

After breakfast I had a new plan. "I want to take a swim," I said.

"Me, too," said Heidi.

"Yeah, why not?" said Ted.

"You can't go in the water until you've digested your breakfast," said my mother.

"I'll go out and wait," I said. When I had pulled open the drapes to let in the morning light, I had seen people sitting around the pool in the distance. Maybe Neal would be there. It was worth a look. I was thinking how nice it would be if we stayed the day and Neal stayed the day. And even another night. I needed more time for Neal to get to know me—for *him* to catch vacation fever. My parents had hoped to spend more than one night in some of the places along the way, so why not this place?

I got my swimsuit out of my suitcase and put it on. Fortunately I don't own a ratty-looking swimsuit, so I couldn't pack one. "See you at the pool," I said, and left before anyone could leave with me. All I had to do was parade over there with my entire family!

There must have been about two dozen people at the pool. Some were swimming, some were splashing in the water, and others were sitting or stretched out at poolside. There were tables with chairs placed around them and there were also separate lounge chairs. The pool area was attractive and bright, an inviting place to spend a few days' vacation.

I was on the watch for Neal. What if his family had checked out? I imagined that some people just check into the motel, spend the night, and leave. Others see it as a place to hang out. I wondered how I could find out if Neal had left. How could I ask at the office in a casual way?

I didn't have to. I recognized a woman sitting at a table. It was Neal's mother. Could I do it? Yes. I walked up to her slowly, figuring I'd get a cold reception. I was not eager to make a fool of myself, but I wanted to know where Neal was. I had to take the chance. She looked at me, but pretended not to recognize me. I knew she knew me, if not from the ketchup incident then from seeing Neal and me talking in the coffee shop last night. "Hello," I said.

"Hello," she said. She was definitely going to play the stranger game.

I wasn't. I decided to be direct. This was the new me. The Vacation Mia. "Where's Neal?"

She really gave me the fish eye. She'd probably lie to me. Neal, she'd say, he's over there with his wife and six children.

"He'll be along," she said.

"Thanks," I said, and walked away. The Vacation Mia faded fast. Mrs. Guest was firmly in her own world of the proper way to do things, and I wasn't going to shake it up. She wasn't a bad-looking woman if your taste runs to cold statues.

I stretched out on a lounge chair. I hoped it wasn't reserved or anything. I saw my parents and Heidi and Ted coming along. I waved. My parents took seats at a nearby table. Ted looked around and then planked himself down next to a teenage girl who was sitting alone at another table. Heidi immediately dived into the water and swam like a fish from one end of the pool to the other. Some of the people around the pool were staring at her. She was an expert swimmer. It was a strange contrast to her other sport of just sitting and watching TV My parents would feel the whole trip was worth it just to get her moving. I envied her. I wished I could streak across the water like that. I would be the subject of admiring eyes, like Neal's when he came along. I began to think his mother had lied to me and he wasn't coming. Maybe he was packing their car to leave.

Then I saw him. I felt nervous. Come on, Vacation Mia, I said to myself. I gave him a bigger wave than I gave my family. I owed him that after not showing up last night. He waved to me, but walked toward the pool and Heidi. He jumped into the pool and swam up to Heidi. Then he and Heidi began to swim in unison up and down the pool. My good old sister Heidi was loving the attention. She was swimming just as powerfully as this older guy. I watched them go back and forth, back and forth. And back and forth, and back and forth. It was going on forever!

At last they both climbed out of the pool. They were laughing. They started to walk back toward the motel, toward our room. Was this the end of it for me? Was Neal after Heidi? She was eleven and he was going into college. He couldn't be in love with her, could he? Do guys do funny things when they're stood up? I had stood him up. He didn't know yet that it wasn't my fault.

Heidi went inside and Neal came back. He headed toward me. This was more like it!

"Hi," he said.

"Hi."

"Your sister's going to be a swimming champ someday."

"Did you tell her that?"

"Yes, and I believe it." He dried himself with a towel. Then he reached for my hand. "Come on, let's escape from the crowd."

"On dry land?" I managed to retort with a smile.

"On dry land."

Escape with Neal. Alone. This really was more like it.

We walked past the pool area and turned down a path. Neal led the way. "There's more to this place than you'd think from the front," he said. "Want to get lost with me?"

I did and I didn't. After all, what did he mean?

We turned down another path. Then he said, "Ah, the perfect tree. Let's sit under it."

He pulled me down beside him. I was a little scared, but it was a nice way to be scared. I started to talk fast. Sometimes I do that when I'm nervous. I said, "I hope you're not angry at me for not showing up last night. Did you figure out why I didn't come? My mother caught me trying to leave the room. Then she decided it was a great night for a stroll for her *and* me. What exactly did she say to you?"

"She talked about crickets, the moon, and what a

beautiful night it was for a stroll. I think she figured out that we had a date. I was standing there as if I were waiting for someone."

"I was dumb enough to mention earlier that I might take a walk outside. I'm sure she remembers you from the ketchup business. I really messed everything up."

"No, you didn't." Neal was looking at me as if he were going to kiss me. And suddenly he did!

Now I knew what Kristi meant about vacation fever. I was in a new place with a new person. It was exciting. It was wonderful. But how long could it last? I was leaving.

"I'm leaving soon," I said. It's a strange thing to say right after someone kisses you. Kind of abrupt, like that was that, and now for the future. But Neal seemed to understand. "Where are you going from here?" he asked.

"We'll be on the road for a few hours, and then spend the night with the family of my mother's roommate in college. Mom hasn't seen her for about ten years. She's got a big house and she offered to put all of us up. How about you?"

"Tonight we'll be just at another motel, but tomorrow night we're staying in Old Southwest. It's a theme park built to look like the Southwest of a hundred years ago. It cost millions and millions of dollars to recreate the streets and buildings authentically. Supposedly you can walk down any street there and feel that you're back into another century. My parents and I are interested in history. I'm familiar with the history of New Mexico and I'm eager to see this place. I just hope it's not a rip-off."

Neal sounded smart. He was good-looking *and* brainy. I liked that combination.

He went on. "My parents are high-school history teachers, and they're curious about this kind of thing. Some other teachers have seen it and said not to miss it. And as long as we're passing nearby . . ."

"Your parents are high-school history teachers? So are mine."

"No kidding. Do you suppose they belong to the same organizations—maybe even know some of the same people?"

I shrugged. "I guess it's possible."

"We should introduce them."

"I suppose." I wasn't sure that I wanted our parents to get friendly. What if Neal's mother started making remarks about me? I was afraid that Neal was going to get up and rush away to make the introductions. But he didn't.

He was staring at me. "I hardly know anything about you," he said. "I'm starting college soon. I already told you that, but how about you, Mia Fisher? Tell me the story of your life. Please."

"I'm starting my senior year in high school, and I'm afraid there's no time for the story of my life."

Neal nodded. "There's so much to talk about and we'll be leaving in a few hours. But I want to keep in touch with you. Let's exchange addresses. Give me your home address and the address you'll be at in Dallas."

"I'll only be in Dallas a week," I said.

"But you'll know I haven't forgotten you if you receive a postcard from me. I love mail, don't you?"

"Guys aren't good about things like that," I said. But I reached into the ratty-looking pocketbook I had with me. I pulled out a pencil stub and a crumpled saleslip. I tore the saleslip in two. "The only paper I've got." I laughed awkwardly. "I'll write my two addresses on the back of my half, and you write your home address on the back of your half. Unless there's a place where I can send you a card on your vacation, too."

"I'll be at a guest ranch in New Mexico for a few nights. I'll write down the address and dates."

Neal and I exchanged two addresses each. As he wrote his down, I wondered how he could be so cool. He must have girls in his life, and he was used to this. But what if he had one special girl? He *must* have. I wouldn't hear from him. I began to worry. Kristi warned me about vacation romances. While you're together, nobody else exists. But once you separate, the magic could dissolve. Vacation romances usually lead to instant dissolve.

Neal was looking at my addresses. "It would be great if we could see each other again on this vacation," he said. "We're going in the same direction."

"But after tonight at my mother's friend's house, I don't know *where* we'll be staying. We don't reserve ahead like your parents. My mother insists on making her motel selections along the way."

"Maybe you could talk her into going to Old Southwest. They have a place to stay right on the grounds and it's supposed to be pretty nice. That's where we're staying. Hey, let's introduce our parents. It couldn't hurt." Abruptly, Neal stood up. He pulled me up. I didn't want to leave, but what could I do?

We walked to the pool area. I hung back. I didn't want to have anything to do with the introduction.

"It'll be all right. I promise," said Neal. "Wait here."

Neal walked to the table where his mother was now sitting with his father. He pointed to my parents sitting at another table. His father got up and walked toward my parents. He spoke to them. Then my parents got up and joined Neal's parents. Without resorting to borrowing a container of ketchup, they met.

Heidi was back in the pool. I had a hunch that Neal's remark about her becoming a champ inspired her. Heidi, liberated from her TV set, was a new person. Ted was doing his usual Ted—getting cozy with a car or a girl. The girl he was sitting with appeared to be in her early teens. She was smoothing her swimsuit as if she were getting used to a new body. She seemed unsure of herself. She was smiling like crazy at Ted. It would be hard getting him to leave this place now. I didn't want to leave, either. All we had ahead of us today were a few hours of travel. That's really why my parents had agreed to stick around the motel longer.

My parents were busy chatting with Neal's parents while Neal stood and watched. His mother was leaning across the table, smiling and talking to my father.

She was definitely capable of civilized conversation. My mother looked dwarfed sitting beside her, her chubby little-doll hands fiddling with a pair of sunglasses. Neal's mother seemed to have a lot to say to my father. Neal's father seemed to be in a world of his own.

Neal was coming back toward me. I noticed how lean and graceful he looked in his dark-red swim trunks. I knew I liked him better than Mack or Phil or Cal. Did I feel such a pull toward him simply because he was a novelty? We were on vacation, I was a new person to him, he was a new person to me. No, it was more than that. I really cared. But how long could it last?

Neal was grinning. "They're hitting it off," he said. "They have an old friend in common. That is, my mother knows an old friend of your father's. Some guy named Alfie Mink."

"I know him. I mean, I know of him. Dad talks about him a lot. Dad and he were buddies years and years ago. My mother met him once and couldn't stand him."

"Incredible. My mother thinks he's a great guy. Anyway our folks are hitting it off as if they've been pals forever."

"Forever's about to end," I said. "My mother's standing up. I guess this is it. We're leaving."

Neal bent down and kissed me again, right in public. I didn't want to leave. Ever. I wondered if his mother saw. I wondered if my parents saw.

Ted was still with the girl. Heidi was still in the

pool. Maybe they would refuse to leave. We could make a stand. Still, Neal was leaving today. Maybe we would meet again. It really was possible.

"Good-bye," I said. "Don't forget to write like you promised." I couldn't help it. I wanted to be cool, but I had to remind him.

I turned and hurried back to my room. Neal had told me that he loved mail. I had just enough time to write a quick postcard to him and send it to the ranch. Time, but no stamps! I left postage money on the card with a note to the chambermaid. She would mail it. I was sure that guests did that all the time.

We were on the road in half an hour.

Dear Kristi,
    This card will be late because I had
to write one to N.G. first. Who is
N.G.? Think V.F. and you'll figure it
out!

                        Mysteriously,
                        Mia

5

We had to practically drag Ted into the car. He
didn't say anything about the girl, but anyone who
could keep him away from a car must have been important. He forgot to nag my father again about driving. Heidi's hair was damp and she kept leaning on
me. She smelled of the swimming pool. But for a
change, she looked like a bright, healthy little crea-
ture, and the pool smell wasn't unpleasant.

"Hi-ho, hi-ho, it's off to Lizette's we go!" My father
was practically singing. He was refreshed, as if he
were just starting the entire trip. He must have found
his conversation with Neal's parents stimulating.
From a distance it had looked to me as if Neal's
mother had talked a blue streak to him. I guess
there's nothing like getting attention, no matter how
old you are. I should know. I had just gotten attention
from the opposite sex and I felt great. I don't understand how I ever could have suspected Neal of giving

me a phony name. He was not only Neal Guest, but my parents were now referring to his parents as Arnold and Hester. It was looking good for me to make a pitch for a reunion at Old Southwest. But I wasn't going to say anything yet. The focus now was on our upcoming visit to my mother's college friend, Lizette Trumbull.

"You'll all love her," my mother said to the back seat.

"Yuck!" said Heidi.

"Lizette's not a food, is she, Mom?" said Ted.

Ted was in a joking mood. Something good must have happened with the girl. Maybe she had told him he was wonderful. Insecure girls are quick with compliments. I wondered if Ted had exchanged addresses.

"I'm going to throw up," said Heidi.

"Oh, no!" said my mother. "What makes you think so?"

"It just feels like it."

"We can't stop now. We just turned into the freeway. Here. Take this plastic bag."

My mother carries plastic bags in her pocketbook. She handed one to Heidi. "Now don't put it on your mouth. That's dangerous. Just hold it below."

"It's your fault," said Heidi. "You made me finish all the milk in the carton. Why couldn't I have coffee?"

"You didn't drink the entire carton of milk," said my mother. "We put some milk in our coffee and Ted had a cup."

"I think it was spoiled," said Ted.

My mother turned to my father. "Did you check the expiration date on the carton before you bought it?"

"No, I didn't think about it. I knew we'd be drinking the milk right up."

"You mean I would," said Heidi. "Oh, I think I'm going to, I think I'm going to. . . ." Heidi paused. "It's passing, it's passing."

"Do you feel sick, Ted?" my mother asked. "If you both feel sick, there was probably something wrong with that milk. We'll have to stop at an emergency room. Spoiled milk is no joke."

"I'm okay," said Ted.

"Sure. Because you spent all your time with that girl," said Heidi. "If you weren't thinking about that girl, maybe you'd feel like throwing up, too."

"Don't be fresh, Heidi," said my mother. "Now, are you sick or are you not sick?"

"I think I'm not sick anymore, but I can't promise for the future."

My mother turned and faced the front. "Well, let me know if the sick feeling comes back."

"She will," said Ted.

I was sitting quietly between Ted and Heidi. The seat was getting to be my home. The movement of the car, the scenery, the cars passing us, our passing other cars, the trucks, the recreational vehicles that came and went, the feeling of the car upholstery, Ted on one side of me, Heidi on the other, the view of the backs of my parents' heads, it was my new life. Was this the vacation that would cause Kristi to choke with envy?

We were now in New Mexico. It was flat out there. The real drama was on the road. There were exciting games to be played. For example, there was a little orange car that passed us. A few miles later, we passed the little orange car. Then, farther along, the little orange car showed up again.

"Didn't we pass that orange car a few miles back?" my mother asked.

What excitement! We were all drawn into the game of whether the orange car would reappear. If it kept passing us and we kept passing it, were all those passings neutralized? My father was a steady driver and so, it appeared, was the driver of the orange car. It wasn't a race, it was a . . . What was it? It was a silly diversion for bored people. I was seventeen years old and I could think of better games to play. I looked at most of the cars as they went by us or we went by them. Why couldn't I remember what Neal's car looked like? I had only seen it in the parking lot of the restaurant, and it wasn't important to me then. The possibility of seeing him on the road kept me awake. But we had left the motel before him, so he was probably way behind us.

It was warm in the car. The air-conditioner was having trouble battling the desert heat. Ted had offered to examine the air-conditioner from time to time, but my father turned him down.

Ted was saving money to buy his own car. He had

an allowance and he took odd jobs in our neighborhood. I hated to think what kind of car he could buy
with the money he had saved. Still, he was attracted
to the challenge of fixing up a relic. He would probably have a chance to face the challenge.

My mother felt obliged to point out and describe
the scenery. Occasionally we'd pass a cluster of
houses or a little town or something she considered
quaint. She got especially excited when we'd see a
dumpy-looking house that someone had fixed up with
great imagination and care. In a way it was interesting because it made you think about the people who
lived in the house and what they were like. Becoming
aware of the way other people live is supposed to be
one of the big rewards of going on vacation, and this
especially appealed to my mother the schoolteacher.

I was thinking of another reward: Neal. The vacation had picked up for me, but I wouldn't admit it to
my parents. How could I say that I liked the vacation
better because I had met a guy? It would sound as if
nothing else mattered. A vacation wasn't supposed to
be a guy. It was supposed to be an experience.

My father pulled into a gas station. While the tank
was being filled, we all got out and stretched. It was
hot. We got soda from a machine and stood around
drinking. Then it was time to get back into the car.

Suddenly I said, "I don't want to sit in the middle
anymore. Ted, you sit in the middle."

"But, Mia, the middle has always been your place,"
said my mother.

"Don't tell me what my place is, Mom! Don't tell

me where to sit. I'm grown up. I can sit where I want, I can go out at night if I want, I can do anything I want."

"The heat's got her," said Heidi.

"And you, Heidi," I said, turning toward her, "if you didn't eat so much, you wouldn't throw up."

"I didn't throw up," Heidi said proudly.

My father put his hand on my shoulder. "Look, being cooped up in a car can get on anyone's nerves. Let's just take it easy. We'll be at Lizette's soon and we'll all have a nice change and plenty of room. Okay?"

I nodded. What alternative did I have anyway? I couldn't stand in front of a hot dusty gas station for the rest of my life. Ted got into the car ahead of me and sat in the middle. Just like that. He was, from time to time, a reasonable person.

We were on the road again.

"Are we there yet?" Heidi asked after fifteen minutes.

"No," said my mother. "How do you feel?"

"I feel like swimming," said Heidi. "My new friend Neal says I'm going to be a champ. He's older and he knows. Can we swim at the place where we're going? Does your friend Lizette have a pool?"

"I really don't know," said my mother. "But please keep in mind that when you stay at someone's home, it's not like a motel."

"You mean Dad won't have to go out and buy breakfast at the supermarket?" Heidi giggled.

"I mean, please treat everything with respect.

Lizette married a successful man, their home is probably full of expensive furniture, so please don't put your feet up on anything or walk around with food or drinks."

My father chuckled. "Brace yourselves, kids. We're going to see how the rich folks live."

Dear Kristi,
You would have been extremely
proud of me for two minutes today in
front of a hot, dusty gas station.
Vacation Mia

6

For what seemed like the millionth time, my mother treated us to the Lizette Trumbull Story. She and Lizette had been roommates in college. After college my mother got married and went into teaching. Lizette got married and that was that. Her husband, Ford, became a big executive in a fruits-and-vegetables empire. His company turns fruits and vegetables into frozen products. Over the years Lizette wrote letters about her big house and exciting trips abroad. Sometimes she mentioned her children: Cecile, who was fourteen, and Nicholas, who was a few months older than me. Mom and Lizette had gotten married around the same time.

I was bored hearing about this Lizette. I'd never met her. Her house was about fifty miles round trip out of our way on our trip, but this was nothing compared to all the miles we were traveling.

"What if Lizette isn't really rich and lives in a

shack?" I asked my mother as we drove into Lizette's town.

"Really Mia, she has enough room in the shack to put all of us up," said my mother. Then she frowned. "Oh, dear, I hope I remembered to pack the presents. I bet I forgot them. I had something for Lizette and her husband and the children."

"She probably doesn't need anything, Mom," I said.

"Yeah, she sounds like she should be giving us stuff," said Ted.

"Now you're *positive* you're not sick, Heidi," said my mother. "If you throw up in Lizette's house, I'll just be so embarrassed."

"I'm perfect," said Heidi.

"That'll be the day," said Ted.

"And, Ted," said my mother, "that reminds me. Please don't go chasing after her daughter. She isn't bold like that girl you met by the pool today."

"How do you know what that girl at the motel is like? You didn't meet her. She's neat. Lizette's daughter is probably a creep because parents' friends' daughters usually are."

"No remarks, Ted." My mother was serious. "Also don't play down the house we live in when we're at Lizette's. It's a good house."

My mother's ego was showing and it hardly ever showed. She obviously felt competitive toward Lizette and she didn't know it.

When we finally arrived, I tried not to be impressed. Lizette's house was a huge two-story brick building with two columns guarding the front porch. We had to drive up a circular path to get there. It was a private path and it was about half a mile long. I expected a butler to come out and greet us. But Lizette came. She had a thin, pale face, black pinned-up hair, and she walked like a ballerina. She was wearing a black dress and long, dangling earrings. She looked like a city person, someone you might expect to see in the middle of New York City. I know a few rich people in the Southwest, but they all live rich in the Southwest style. Expensive jeans, horses, sprawling houses, a kind of low-slung, spread-out atmosphere. Lizette looked high-rise rich.

My mother and Lizette squealed and hugged each other, just like teenagers. Then Lizette hugged the rest of us. She was so thrilled to meet us. I felt skeptical. She had never come to visit us in all these years. And perhaps if she lived seventy-five or a hundred miles out of the way on this trip, we wouldn't have visited her. This joyous meeting might never have taken place if it weren't convenient, and yet it was being treated as if it were a milestone in all our lives.

She led us into the house. She said her butler would take care of our luggage. I *knew* there was a butler. But when I caught sight of him later, he was dressed in a blue workshirt and jeans and he had grease on him. He looked like a handyman. Since Lizette had called him a butler, I wondered about Lizette.

She did, however, have a maid who looked like a maid, and a son and daughter who stood waiting to meet us. Nicholas and Cecile were strained and polite when we were introduced, as if they had been coached in advance. Nicholas offered to carry my suitcase and show me to my room.

The room was decorated in blue and white, with a blue-and-white bedspread, matching drapes, a matching chair, and I suddenly noticed, a matching ceiling. I tried not to notice. I remembered what my mother had said about not playing down the house we live in. If I raved about this house too much, it would be like saying my own wasn't that great. Something about being in this house and meeting Lizette made me feel loyal to my mother, closer to her.

Nicholas put my suitcase down. "I've got a rock band," he announced.

"What?" I had expected him to say something about the room, and I was prepared to say, Yes, it's a very nice room. What could I say about a rock band I had never heard, and why was he telling me this anyway?

He went on. "I have a large collection of tapes and records in my room. Want to see them?"

He was waiting for my answer. He looked amazingly like his mother, with his dark hair and pale face. He really wanted to show me his things.

"Sure," I said.

I followed Nicholas down the hall to his room. It was even nicer than mine. It was decorated in various shades of brown. A gorgeous stereo dominated the room, and there were books and records everywhere. There were shelves and nooks for everything. The room was perfectly neat. It's easier to be neat when you're rich.

"Great room," I said.

"You like it? Thanks. This is where I compose. I'm a songwriter as well as a singer. My parents hate that. They expect me to go to an Ivy League college, but I'm going on the road with my group when I finish high school. My mother went to college and all she did was marry a rich man. All of my friends are rich. Are you rich? You don't look it, but not looking it is one of the affectations of the rich."

"I'm not rich." I didn't want to go any further than that. I was doing more than obeying my mother's instructions. I was creating and obeying some of my own. I was feeling like part of my family unit, that I was one of the visiting Fishers, and I couldn't blab the story of my life. I was feeling lonely for my comfortable room in this rich brown room.

Nicholas was eager to confide in me. "My group is called Nicholas and Dimes. There's one Nicholas and five Dimes. We have silver costumes. I'm the lead singer. We do mostly protest songs."

"Isn't protest out of date? I mean, the songs."

"It's coming back. Anyway our families thought the group was a nice little hobby, but now they hate it because we're serious about it. One of the kids has a van and we travel. Not very far, not yet. I'm earning my own money. I will never be a parasite. Want to hear the lyrics of a song I just wrote? It's called

'Materialism.' Are you sure you're not rich? Are you a fat cat? Because if you are, I won't sing them for you."

"No, I'm not a fat cat. Do you see whiskers and a tail?"

Nicholas laughed. I was getting the feeling that he liked me. He wanted to share his song with me. He was telling me all kinds of things about himself. This rich guy was attracted to me. What would Neal think? If only he could see Nicholas and me together . . . Maybe he would think that Nicholas was a little weird. But that's okay because it's okay to be weird when you're rich. It's only when you're poor that you have to be as normal as possible.

Nicholas started to sing his song. He didn't know that my ego was soaring as high as the notes of his song.

Every day when I wake up, I bow down at the shrine
And thank whichever god made my Mercedes mine,
all mine.
I have a bunch of credit cards to verify my worth,
They bulge from all my pockets and increase my total
girth.
Materialism! Ya! Ya! Ya!
My neighborhoods were boring when I didn't have a
dime,
Now I live next door to Big Boss, who's reorganizing
crime.
Materialism! Ya! Ya! Ya!

"Nicholas." The maid was standing at the door.

"Dinner will be served in five minutes." She smiled and left.

Nicholas continued his song as if he hadn't been interrupted. He had a terrific voice. I could imagine him in his silver suit in front of an audience.

There are haves and there are have nots, the have nots live in cars
Inevitably repossessed by men with fat cigars.
Materialism! Ya! Ya! Ya!
Beggars stop me in the street and ask me for a quarter,
It wrecks the beauty of my day, I just don't think they oughta.
To give my money to the poor is totally sadistic
It gives them hope they have the right to be—materialistic!
When day is done and shadows fall
I thank the Lord I have it all.
Materialism! Ya! Ya! Ya!

"Well?" Nicholas was waiting. He wanted *my* opinion. It counted. He appreciated me. Maybe a person has to go on vacation to meet new people in order to be really appreciated. Maybe by now in Phoenix I'd be like a loaf of stale bread.

"It's great," I said. "I really like it."

"You should hear it with three of us doing vocals and the synthesizer and the guitars. We're making a tape and sending it around. I'll mail you a tape, okay?"

"Sure, I'd love it. Thanks."

"My mother has your address, right?"

"Right."

I knew Nicholas wouldn't forget to send the tape. I was certain Nicholas wouldn't forget me. I felt kind of sorry for him. He didn't belong in this house. He didn't want to live rich. That's because he'd never been poor, or even in the middle. How would he like to be the son of two schoolteachers in a modest neighborhood with a modest car? I could never write a song like his. I was coming from somewhere else.

I wondered if Nicholas had any girlfriends. He was acting like someone who didn't. Maybe I should tell him I have a boyfriend. But I wasn't sure I did. I didn't know what to do or say.

"You're cute," he said suddenly.

"Oh, well, thanks."

"Do all the guys tell you that?"

"Well . . ."

"Maybe just one particular guy tells you that?"

"There is kind of one particular guy I met on this trip."

"On a car trip? We never take car trips. We take jets and we travel on yachts and stuff. Do you have to be poor to take a car trip? What's it like? The guy you met, does he pump gas or something?"

"No. I really don't know him very well."

"Oh, then it's a romancy romance. Absolutely terrible songs are written about romancy romances. They don't last, you know."

I didn't want to hear that. I changed the subject. "Do you date anybody special?"

"I used to date one of the Dimes. Nothing heavy. My parents hassled me about it. They approved of this girl when she wasn't a Dime. But when she put on that silver suit—wham! they got disgusted. They should get disgusted over my sister, Cecile. She's extremely boy-crazy, and that's the understatement of the century."

"Did you like this Dime?"

Nicholas laughed. "No, I'm really looking to fall in love with a quarter. You look like a quarter to me. I meant it when I said you're cute. I'm sincere. Even though I'm rich, I'm sincere."

"I know it."

"My father will fly me anywhere in the world that I want. He'd fly me to Phoenix. I don't approve of doing rich things, you know, but for you I'd do it."

"Oh?" I didn't know what to say. It all sounded so *jet set!* Neal, are you listening to this? Of course you're not listening to this! But how I wish you were.

The maid appeared at the door again.

"Okay, okay," Nicholas said, and we walked down the stairs to dinner. "Think about what I said," he whispered to me.

"I will."

I had an overwhelming desire for Nicholas to be happy. I have this musical girlfriend, Doreen, who lives in Mesa, Arizona. Possibly she could make Nicholas happy. First thing she'd do is call him Nick. I think he needs that.

We walked into the dining room. I guess we were late because everyone was looking up at us as if they had been waiting. We sat down. Lizette's husband, Ford, had come home and was sitting at the head of the rectangular table. My mother was on his right, then my father, and then Lizette. Across from my mother and father were Heidi, Nicholas, and me. Cecile and Ted were missing.

"I gather Cecile is showing Ted around the grounds," said Ford Trumbull. "They probably got lost." He smiled as he acknowledged the immense size of the grounds of his house.

Nicholas also smiled. He was acknowledging the possibility that Cecile and Ted were lost on purpose. "A nymphomaniac," he whispered to me. "My four-teen-year-old sister's a nympho."

Lizette sat there, serene and poised, as if her family were nice and normal. Ford, whom I was seeing for the first time, was about twenty years older than her. He had an accent I couldn't place. He turned to my father and started to talk about stocks and bonds. My mother was sitting next to him, but he was speaking to my father. He had to ignore my mother to do this. He wanted to have a man-to-man conversation. It was the way he did things. It wasn't the way my father did them. My father said simply that he and my mother owned a few stocks and bonds jointly.

Ford didn't have a chance to reply. Ted and Cecile suddenly appeared in the dining room. Ted had a smirky smile on his face. Cecile did a little hop and skip.

"Not in the dining room, Cecile," said Lizette.

Cecile and Ted sat down at the table.

"I was just looking at one of your cars," Ted said.

Nicholas nudged me. "From the inside, with Cecile, I'll bet." He was careful to whisper.

"You know something about cars, young man?" asked Ford.

"Plenty. I'm going to be a mechanic someday."

"A mechanic? You mean a mechanical engineer?" asked Lizette.

"No, a mechanic," said Ted.

"Oh," said Lizette.

The dull "oh" was not lost on my mother.

But it was Heidi who spoke up. "What's wrong with being a mechanic? Ted can fix anything in a car. He's a genius."

Heidi was sticking up for our brother. No matter how many wisecracks and insults passed between them, they were brother and sister. And when an outsider insulted one, the other was insulted, too. My mother was silent. Was it dawning on her, finally, that she and Lizette had been going in opposite directions for years? Before she could say anything, Lizette tried to cover up the awkward moment.

"Well, how did we get so serious?" Lizette asked. She took a hot roll from a sterling-silver tray. "More rolls anyone?"

The food was delicious, but I didn't recognize what it was. It seemed to be disguised. I hoped it wasn't too fancy for Heidi. What if she got sick again? I looked around for the most exquisite piece of furniture for Heidi to get sick over.

Ford started to talk about what a great year he'd had in business. It was so great they were all going to the Riviera in the fall. It was his present to Lizette and the children. Lizette's whole life seemed to be a present from Ford. That was their setup and they both seemed content with it.

"Money means nothing to us and everything to us," said Nicholas.

"Nicholas!" Lizette was furious.

My mother laughed nervously, as if Nicholas had been kidding. Here we were, sitting around a beautiful table, getting a delicious free meal served on gorgeous china with sterling silverware. Tonight we would go to sleep in lovely rooms. We were reaping the rewards of a friendship that had begun over twenty years ago. I felt sorry for my mother, since this great friendship had died along the way without anyone finding out until now.

Dear Kristi,
    Somebody rich, talented, and future-famous loves me. It is okay to share this postcard.

Loving it,
Mia

7

We took pictures with my parents' camera in front of the big house before we left. All kinds of friendly poses and combinations. Lizette and Mom. Lizette and Ford and Mom and Dad. The entire two families together, taken by the maid. I snapped one of the maid and Nicholas. Lizette looked puzzled, but Nicholas and I just smiled. I took one of Ted and Cecile. Ted almost blushed. We promised to send copies of all the pictures. We all hugged as enthusiastically as when we had arrived because that's the way things are done no matter how you feel.

As we drove down the circular driveway away from the house, everyone was still waving. I knew we would never come back. If we were a mile away, we'd never come back. It was time for our vacation to start again. This stop was and was not part of it. Whether Mom and Lizette would keep up their correspondence, I didn't know. I was sure Mom would send a thank-you note and a gift. The gifts she had bought in advance hadn't shown up. There hadn't been any fight between Lizette and her. It was as if they had finally taken inventory and found they had been stocking different kinds of merchandise all these years.

I thought of all the film we had wasted on our hypocritical snapshot session. It reminded me that I could have taken pictures of Neal. I hadn't even thought of it. If I never saw him again or heard from him again, at least I would have had some pictures.

It was time to work on my plan for seeing him again. "Where do we go from here?" I asked.

"The Guests, the parents of that young man you met, were raving about this historical theme park, Old Southwest. Their friends told them it's not to be missed." My mother had turned around to talk to me. Was she about to give me a pitch for going to meet Neal? I could have hugged her.

"So we're going?"

"Yes," said my father. "We're on our way. Arnold Guest gave me directions."

I settled back in my seat blissfully. I didn't have to beg or anything. I couldn't believe how easy it was.

"Hooray!" said Ted. "At last we're gonna do fun."

"Your friend Lizette isn't much fun, Mom," Heidi said. "She didn't even let us use her pool. The person who's fun is Neal Guest."

My mother was facing front. She stayed that way. "Let's not talk about someone who fed us and gave us shelter for the night."

72

"Why not?" said Ted. "We talk about crummy motels. This was just a fancy crummy place. A mechanical *engineer!* Where does she get off?"

"I don't want to discuss it, Ted."

My mother's choice of a friend was now something to be talked about in the family. My mother, who always cautioned us to choose our friends wisely, had landed up with a boo-boo of a friend herself.

"What a wimp!" said Ted.

"Yeah, she's the second unpleasant lady we've met on this trip," I said. "Mrs. Guest has competition."

"Lizette is not a wimp, whatever that is," said my mother. "She simply lives a different kind of life than we do."

"You just don't want to admit that you have bad taste," said Ted.

"Ted, be quiet!" My mother raised her voice.

My father half-turned toward Ted while he tried to keep his eyes on the road. "Ted, I am trying to watch the road. My palms are sweaty, my eyes are bleary, the traffic's heavy, and I didn't sleep last night. They had a cuckoo clock in our room."

My mother kind of bowed her head as if this were crushing evidence that Lizette was a bad friend. It just struck me as stupid to put a cuckoo clock in a guest room.

My father went on. "That remark about Mrs. Guest wasn't fair, Mia. Would you believe she knows that old friend of mine, Alfie Mink? It's a small world. Hester and I had a very pleasant time reminiscing. She had some great stories."

"I wouldn't reminisce about Alfie Mink," said my mother. "I'd try to forget him. I never liked him. He was a bad influence on you, Hugh. I can't understand why Hester Guest would pump you for information about him, as if there were anything worth knowing."

"Just a minute, Gwen. When it comes to old friends, your taste isn't exactly perfect. The kids aren't wrong about Lizette."

"Lizette was a sweet and modest person when she was in college," said my mother. "She's changed, that's all. Is it my fault that she changed?"

"If you had taken the trouble, made a little effort to know Alfie, you'd have a different opinion of him," my father continued.

"Enough!" said my mother. She was almost screaming.

My father's knuckles tightened around the steering wheel. We were having a family fight. In the car. On a busy highway.

Heidi spoke up. "Are we there yet?"

"Where?" asked my father.

"You know, that Old Southwest place."

"It's miles and miles away," said my father. "Just relax."

Everything quieted down. Heidi had gotten us back to normal.

My father was anxious to do as much driving as he could before stopping for lunch. He was afraid his lack of sleep would affect him more and more as the day went on. I offered to drive, but Dad was so protective of his car he said, "No, thanks." Ted got a bigger "No."

We had lunch in the middle of the afternoon. We pulled up to a place that looked like an old-fashioned cottage, the kind that people were once supposed to live happily ever after in. It was called KOZEE KITCHENS or something like that. I don't care for just plain adorable. Still, it kind of charmed me. Even Ted noticed it. He gave a little whistle. A picket fence had been built across the front of the eating section. Customers entered through a swinging gate in the middle. There were green-and-white polka-dotted curtains and tablecloths. It seemed as if we had left Lizette's house behind in another world and we were back on our vacation. *Our* vacation? Was I beginning to think that way? I was.

All of us except Heidi ordered an egg dish with a cute name. Heidi had a tuna special. My father yawned a few times during the meal.

"How much longer to go?" I asked.

"About two hours."

"That's not too bad. Think you can hold out?"

"Sure."

"I'll be glad to drive," I said again.

"Me, too," Ted piped up.

My father smiled. "I'm handling the driving on this trip. But thanks, kids."

The meal in the little polka-dotted cottage was the nicest we'd had so far. Of course, it would have been nicer if Neal and his family had walked in, but I knew that was just my fantasy and an impossible reality.

Ted had managed to get rid of a lot of his hostility by taking it out on the memory of Lizette and, unfortunately, on my mother. But the vacation was going pretty well for him even if he wouldn't admit it. The girl back at the motel had liked him, I could tell. And Cecile . . . well, possibly he had a mind-blowing experience with her. He wasn't talking. I was actually glad I had come on the vacation. I couldn't wait to see Neal again. As for Heidi, she hadn't mentioned TV in quite a while. She had found Lizette's house an adventure. She was the youngest and she didn't require as much from her adventures. She was satisfied to have been waited on by a maid and to have had her own guest room, which she reported to us was yellow and white everywhere you looked. She loved her taste of stardom at the motel pool as she swam back and forth. Guests talked about her. Neal praised her. Back home everyone already knew she was a talented swimmer. Ahead of her on vacation might be more pools and more admiration.

Back on the road again, we must have traveled for about an hour when my father said the fatal words, "Oh no!"

"Oh no, what?" asked Heidi.

"I missed our exit."

"We'll just have to go back a bit," said my mother. "We don't mind."

"No. It's not a bit. I just realized we wanted the exit that was only a mile or so beyond the restaurant."

"How could you miss it?" I asked. "Aren't they numbered?"

"Yes, but they're confusing. And having a cuckoo-clock hangover doesn't help."

"But we'll go back and pick up the exit, right? All of us will watch for it this time."

"It might be more complicated than that. The directions Arnold gave me seem clear on paper, but I don't know. I thought the exit after we left the restaurant said east, which didn't seem right to me. Well, I'll have to go back and try it. West is obviously wrong. It'll take about an hour."

"Oh, man!" said Ted.

"I don't understand," said my mother. "Are we lost anyway or are we just lost as far as finding Old Southwest?"

"Old Southwest," said my father. "It's about twelve miles off the road, which is no sweat in itself. We're on the wrong road. It's way back there . . . somewhere."

"So," said my mother, "if we just keep on this road, we're fine." She spoke as if she'd just simplified a complex problem. "We'll proceed with our trip and try to see Old Southwest on the way back."

"But it won't be the same," I said.

Ted looked at me as if I were crazy. But then he grinned at me and said, "I want to see it now. If you think about it, we haven't seen one real attraction since we started this trip."

"We'll vote," said my father. "I'm willing to do whatever the rest of you want to do."

"I think you're too tired to drive one extra mile out of the way," said my mother. "I vote that we continue on and don't go back."

"Old Southwest!" said Ted.

"Old Southwest!" said Heidi.

The vote was two for, one against going to Old Southwest. Of course I knew how I was going to vote!

"Well," said my father.

I thought of the miles and miles we had traveled since we left the polka-dotted cottage restaurant. I thought about the cuckoo clock and my father's fatigue. I thought about making him go back and trying to find the right exit. But more than anything I thought about his willingness to do it even though he was dead tired. I couldn't make him do it. I just couldn't. "Straight ahead," I said. "That's my vote."

Ted and Heidi groaned. I had more to groan about than they did. Who knows what would have happened if I saw Neal again? Maybe we were on the brink of falling in love. Now there was a tie vote. Two for going ahead, two for turning back. My father wasn't voting. I knew how the tie was going to be broken. My mother's vote was the most important one. As Kristi had told me, kids were out*aged* by parents.

I hoped I wasn't afraid to face Neal again and that's why I voted for my dad. I did want to see Neal again but not at my father's expense. The Vacation Mia I was trying to be was really just Mia.

"Straight ahead, Hugh," my mother said. Then she sighed. I could see that she was truly sorry about how

78

things turned out. She turned around and looked at us sympathetically.

"That Lizette and her stupid, hand-carved, pretentious cuckoo of a cuckoo clock!"

It was my *mother* talking.

We didn't mention Lizette again, not once for the rest of the trip.

"We'll have a wonderful vacation yet," my mother added, and turned on the car radio.

Dear Kristi,
Cuckoo clocks should be banished
from the face of the earth.
Heartbroken Mia

8

My mother offered us a "real" consolation prize for missing Old Southwest. A resort motel for the night, if we could find one with a vacancy. "Something with a beautiful pool, and tennis courts, and a recreation room, and a spa and a dining room, something really snazzy."

"Don't get your hopes up," said my father. "Places like that are usually reserved in advance. But be on the lookout for signs. No harm in trying."

"We're entering a resort area," said my mother. "Now everybody watch."

My mother was trying so hard to make up for the loss of Old Southwest. She and my father may have dragged Ted and Heidi and me along on this vacation, but they did want us to enjoy it. They were, in their own way, making a brave effort.

We checked into a huge motel complex that had artificial ponds in addition to a giant swimming pool and other attractions. The reservations clerk told us we were fortunate because they had just had a cancellation for two adjoining rooms. He obviously wanted us to understand that you couldn't just drive in off the streets and expect to be put up in an exclusive place like this. The rooms turned out to be spacious, with floor-to-ceiling windows, and pretty enough for Heidi to say "Wow!"

After we unpacked, my parents decided to take a nap while Heidi, Ted, and I headed for the pool. Heidi immediately went into the water, and Ted sat down in a chair near the pool. I headed for an empty lounge chair at the other end. I didn't want to cramp Ted's style by staying with him. I suppose I didn't want to cramp my style either. But as I looked around, it seemed to me that this was mostly a family place. Lots of kids splashing in the shallow end of the pool.

I stretched out on the lounge chair. Part of the afternoon was still left, the sun was shining, and I wanted to get a tan to take back home. Actually I wanted a tan so that if we bumped into Neal again—which I knew was impossible—I'd look like a movie star—which I also knew was impossible! It was easy enough to get a tan back home in Phoenix, but a New Mexico tan was a vacation tan, and a different matter entirely.

I had forgotten my tanning lotion. I felt myself getting thoroughly baked. I turned over and looked around for Ted and Heidi. Heidi was easy. Back and forth, back and forth, she was yet again the star of the swimming pool. Ted had moved. Where was he? I thought I saw him dangling his legs in the pool. I did. But he wasn't alone. He was with an older guy. Someone who looked about twenty. I was glad Ted had found a friend. Should I go over and join them? No, don't butt in. Butt in. What did I have to lose?

I walked over to them slowly. If Ted turned his back and pretended he didn't know me, I'd walk on. He was like that sometimes. Embarrassed to be the younger brother, I guess. But he was beckoning to me. "Hey, Mia, come over and meet my friend Kip. Kip, my sister Mia."

"Hi," I said.

Kip put his hands on his hips and said hi while he looked me over.

I stood there, feeling silly. Was I supposed to walk on?

Kip was very tanned, a little on the short side, solid-looking, with a hairy chest that was the background for a glittering gold chain.

"Kip says this place is a drag," said Ted. "He's been here a few days already. No action."

"It seems to be a family place," I said. I wasn't going to ask Kip to describe his idea of action.

"Kip and I were trying to cook up something for tonight," said Ted. "He's planning a little party in his room."

Kip and I. That's what Ted had said. Up close, Kip looked too old to be a pal for Ted. He seemed seasoned, as if he'd been around. He could be as old as twenty-five. I was waiting for him to invite me to his party, but he didn't.

Even though Kip was a new guy, attractive in a bold, masculine way, I was not really attracted to him. His eyes darted about, sizing things up, always in action. Impatient eyes. Not to be trusted. Neal had appealed to me immediately. He had gentle eyes. Neal's eyes had focused on *me*.

Still, maybe I was being hasty. Back up, Mia. So what if his eyes were impatient? That's not a crime. Why dismiss someone for that?

Kip's eyes settled on me. He was *really* looking me over now. I heard a little voice inside me whisper, Why not? Neal liked me. Nicholas liked me. Kip could like me, too.

Ted said, "I'll be back, you guys," and he walked away.

Kip kept sizing me up. Then he said, "Want to come to the party?"

"Maybe. What kind of party is it? I didn't pack party clothes."

"With your looks, you don't need any clothes." Kip half-smiled.

Was he kidding?

"Do you like to dance?" he asked.

"I love to dance."

"Real close? I mean *real* close. Know what I mean?"

"I'm afraid I do." I started to turn away.

Kip touched my arm. "Did I say something wrong? You're here on vacation, aren't you? If you can't party on vacation, what's life all about?"

83

"I think it's about something you don't understand."

"Ah, you're looking for a fight. Super! I'm turned on by girls who want to fight. Come to the party. You'll be fantastic."

"No, thanks. I'll just stay in my room and be fantastic with my family."

I started to walk back to my room. Ted caught up with me.

"How well do you know Kip?" I asked Ted.

"Ten minutes better than you do. He came up to me and started to talk. But I'm going to his party. Girls! There'll be girls, he promised."

"I hope they're not too old for you."

"Cecile Trumbull was too old for me and she was younger than me."

"Nicholas was right."

"What do you mean?"

"Forget it, Ted. But honestly, I'd think twice about partying with this Kip."

"Are you in training to be a mother?"

I shrugged and walked back to our room. I wasn't thinking about Kip's party. I was thinking about Neal, probably waiting for me at Old Southwest. This would be the second time he'd wait for me without my showing up.

My parents were up and around. "What's the plan for tonight?" I asked. I tried to hide my disappointment at being with them and not Neal.

"We're eating in the dining room here," my mother said. "It's charming. Wait till you see it."

The dining room was charming. It had an inside-outside look with desert plants on view everywhere. Huge windows provided a chance to gaze at the mountains and watch a multicolored sunset while we ate. The hitch was the food. It was mediocre. The prices, however, were as spectacular as the mountains, and as my father observed, "Just as high." After what my parents spent tonight, we'd probably have to eat a supermarket breakfast.

I noticed Kip in a corner of the dining room. He was at a table for two. His clothes were sharp. But he seemed lonely. Maybe he had just been putting on an act for me with all that suggestive party talk. Maybe he thought he was macho, but he was really shy. He was looking my way. I smiled at him. He smiled back, but it was a slick smile. I had been right in the first place.

After dinner we went back to our rooms. The adjoining rooms were a convenient arrangement that allowed us to share supplies easily and to be both together and separate. A cot was supposed to have been brought into one of the rooms, but it hadn't come. My mother said that she and Heidi would sleep in one of the double beds and I could have the other. Heidi was surprisingly agreeable. She was exhilarated from her triumph in the swimming pool.

It was time for a family discussion about what to do for the evening's entertainment. "We're paying a lot of money to stay here," my mother said. "Let's utilize the place."

Accordingly the five of us toured the grounds. Then

we sat by the pool, then inside the busy lobby. Then my mother and father discussed whether or not to play tennis since the courts were there.

"I think I'll watch TV," said my father. He was still tired.

"We can do that at home," said my mother.

"TV," said Heidi. "I want to do that."

We all went back to the rooms to watch TV. Ted plunked himself on a bed, so I guessed that he had decided against going to Kip's party. But after watching half an hour of the local news during which Heidi pointed out all the differences between our local newscasters and the ones here, Ted got up and announced that he was going out.

My mother quickly asked, "Where?"

"I met this kid who's staying here and he invited me over."

"Is it all right with his parents?"

"I guess so."

I looked at the ceiling. Kip was no kid.

"What room is he staying in?"

"Two-eleven."

"Be back by ten. We want to go to bed early."

"Okay."

"Are you sure his parents don't mind?"

"You can count on it."

Ted left. He left me with the responsibility of what to do about him. Kip might be in his mid-twenties, a stranger, a sharp dresser, who knows what. Fifteen-year-old boys can be so dumb. I wanted to go to that party to protect Ted. I didn't have any other reason.

But how could I leave the room? I remembered the last time I tried at night. I could give an innocent-sounding reason like Ted's. But he had already used it up.

I was worried about Ted. Anything could happen on a vacation. People act differently. Now I knew how my mother felt when I went off to what she considered unseen dangers. Is this what happens when you get to be a parent? I watched TV for about an hour while I tried to figure out what to do. It was now dark outside. I wished Ted would come back. I could imagine the kind of girls Kip would invite to a party. The kind who wore purple satin pants and very high heels and gold-lamé shorts. I felt anxious just thinking about clothing.

"Want to take a walk?" I asked my mother.

"No, I don't think so," she said.

"Then I'll go," I said. "I'll be back soon."

"I feel like a walk," said my father.

He felt like guarding me, that's what he felt like. But I didn't care. I felt I had to go out and check on Ted.

It was a cool night. The air felt sensational. It was the kind of night that made me know I was on vacation.

We walked toward the office. I kept looking around as we walked. We passed the recreation video game room on the way. I peered in. I saw the back of a familiar-looking head. It was Ted's. He was sitting at a table with an elderly lady and a boy about ten or twelve. They were playing cards.

We walked out into the refreshing cool night. "I guess Ted's getting old enough to take care of himself," I said, smiling.

"Don't count on it," said my father.

Ted's really something.

Dear Kristi,
How come you didn't warn me
that some of the guys you meet on
vacation aren't worth meeting?
Your disillusioned friend,
Mia

9

It was great climbing into the double bed. I had it all to myself. My mother and Heidi were already asleep in the next bed. My father and Ted were in the next room, probably asleep. Ted had come home soon after my father and I had seen him. I didn't mention my short quest to find him.

The bed was soft. This was a nice motel. It supplied little extras—free shoeshine cloths, free shower caps, soap shaped like a flower. We probably couldn't afford to stay here. Our trip had been carefully budgeted. But this place was a welcome haven when my father was so tired, and besides, it felt good to put a little luxury into our lives. I deserved flower-shaped soap.

Thump!

I heard a sound. Was it a tree stirred up by a breeze or the start of a desert storm? It was fun lying there, listening to nature's sound effects.

Thump. Thump. Thump.

Nature had nothing to do with it. These were footsteps coming from above. And then there were more footsteps. And then, like an explosion, music! Just above my ceiling everything came alive. One minute it was nothing, the next minute all of humanity seemed to be holding a reunion. Shrieks of laughter for jokes unheard. A stampede by feet unseen. What was going on up there? A party, of course. Not Kip's party. It wasn't room 211 upstairs. For a minute I was hopeful that the sounds were caused by just a few pair of feet and a television set. When people travel, they sometimes return to their rooms, blast the TV set to get the news or weather for the next day, scramble around getting ready for bed, and then, as suddenly as it started, the tornado of noise is gone and everyone's settled in peacefully for the night. But the noises above were *beginning* noises. I could tell because they were getting louder. More people must have been arriving upstairs. For them, the evening was young. My mother stirred and woke up.

I whispered, "Mom."

"What's going on? Is the ceiling falling in?"

"Not yet," I said. "I think a party's starting upstairs."

"What time is it?"

"I don't know."

Heidi woke up. "What's happening?"

"I'm going to turn on the light. Ready?" I said. I switched on a lamp and looked at my watch on the bedside table. "It's eleven. Ten past, actually."

"What are they *doing* upstairs?" My mother sat up. "This is a disgrace. How are we supposed to sleep?"

The door to the adjoining room opened. My father, groggy and somewhat astonished, was standing there. "*You* heard it, too? It's just above our ceiling."

"And above ours, too," I said.

"Can we go to the party?" asked Heidi.

"*No!*" My mother was aggravated. "Hugh, should we give them time to settle down or complain right now?"

"Let's give them a little time. Perhaps they're just having a drink together."

"Together, as in an army?" I asked.

"If this place costs so much to stay in," said Heidi, "how come we can hear other people's parties?"

"The builders put the money into eye-catching features," said my father. "And they saved by putting in paper-thin walls and ceilings."

Ted came into the room, and we all sat around in our nightclothes looking so sleepy we must have seemed like a disheveled bunch of survivors waiting to be rescued from something.

The noise upstairs continued.

There was a sound as if something heavy had been dropped on the floor. "They just shot someone out of a cannon," said Ted.

"That does it," said my father. He picked up the telephone and called the front desk. "Someone had better be on duty. Oh, hello. Yes, we're in rooms 156 and 157 and there seems to be a wild party going on just above our two rooms. It's impossible to sleep."

91

My father paused and listened. Then he said, "I know it's not midnight yet. How do you know they'll stop at midnight? Look, we're two weary adult travelers and three children and we're entitled to some peace and quiet." Another pause. "Fine. We appreciate that."

He hung up. "They're calling and asking them to quiet down."

"That's a relief," said my mother. "At least the motel management is responsive. When you stay in one of these better places, you get better management."

"They wanted to wait until midnight," said my father. "I don't call that responsive."

"I can hear their phone ring," said Heidi. "It's just like a television program or a movie."

We waited. I was trying not to be angry that my father called me a child. I guess he did it for effect.

"The music sounds a little lower," I said. "Yes, I think it does."

"Does it?" asked my mother. "Everybody listen."

We all listened. "It may be a little quieter up there," I said. "They're cooperating. I guess most people cooperate if you bring a problem to their attention."

"Are we nuts?" asked Ted. "What if it's a little quieter? It's still blasting."

Ted was right. The party had quieted down about, well, I'm not good at percentages, but I'd guess 5 percent. That meant we were left with only 95 percent noise.

My mother was fuming. "We paid a small fortune

to stay in this noise factory. I want more than flower-shaped soap for my money."

My mother had noticed the soap, too. What did it matter? Soap-shaped soap gets you clean, too. My mother's opinion of this motel was changing fast.

My father picked up the phone again, dialed a number, and waited. "This is Room 156 and 157 calling you once more. They're still blasting away up there." Pause. Then, "I know you called them. We heard their phone ring. But the noise is still intolerable. We can't sleep." Pause. "Very well."

My father hung up. "They'll try again."

We heard the phone ring upstairs. Suddenly everything quieted down. Stopped. A miracle. Our night was saved.

"Children," said my mother, "sometimes people aren't aware that they're infringing upon other people's rights. But when you ask them in a nice way to stop, usually they understand. Most people are decent and cooperative."

My mother's last words, "decent and cooperative," were drowned out by the noise that resumed up above. What probably had happened was that the noise had been turned off just so the telephone conversation could be heard.

My father put on his robe and marched toward the door.

"Where are you going, Dad?" Heidi asked.

We all knew. "Wait!" my mother said. Silently we grabbed our robes. We all wanted to go with my father. The five of us straggled out into the night in our robes and slippers. Ted, Heidi, and I followed our parents to the office. Two men were behind the front desk. One of them asked, "May I help you?" as if we looked normally dressed for the outside world.

"You *could* help us, but you don't seem to be able to," said my father. "As you may have guessed from our attire, we're the people from rooms 156 and 157 who are being bombarded by the noise from above."

"Oh, yes," said one of the men pleasantly.

"Are you the manager?" asked my father.

"I'm the night manager. And we try to help each and every guest who passes through our doors have a pleasant motel experience."

"Is that a fact?" said my father. "Well, tell me, who takes precedence in your establishment? Guests who want to party or guests who want to sleep?"

"We try to satisfy all of our patrons," said the manager.

My mother was getting furious. "Let's cut all the public-relations junk," she said. "Are you going to stop that party or are we going to check out?"

"Perhaps if you understood that the guests above you are part of a convention . . . they hired a block of fifty rooms."

We were outnumbered. It was clear that the management was not going to alienate the occupants of fifty rooms when the alternative was simply to intimidate the occupants of two rooms. Wrecking the sleep of merely five people was not much of a sacrifice for the night manager to make.

"These convention folks come back year after

year," he added. "And if I may say, you're the only ones complaining. Perhaps some hot milk . . ."

"We're checking out," said my father. "We want our money back."

"Your *money*? Really. You've used our facilities, haven't you? You've slept in our beds, haven't you?" The night manager was getting indignant.

"We're entitled to a night's sleep," Ted said. He was getting into the fight and making a good point.

"It's not that simple. Our computer already has you registered as a guest, your credit card has . . ."

My father interrupted again. "I don't own a credit card. I paid cash."

"You did *what?*"

"I paid cash," my father repeated.

"But we're not allowed to take cash," said the manager. "Who was on duty here when you paid cash?"

"An elf," said Heidi. "With green ears."

Our family was so united! Even though we argued a lot at home, we were really together now. I felt like a real daughter, a real sister, a member of a family. Next summer I'd be getting ready for college, for life on my own. I wouldn't be going places with my family. We would never be together like this in quite the same way again. That's what my mother had said when we started the trip. Finally I knew what she meant.

My father's face was about an inch from the manager's. "We want our money," he said. "*Now.* And if you're sizing us up to see if we're bright enough to know what authorities to complain to, I can save you the trouble. We are. We will write an irate letter to the chairman of the board of this chain of motels explaining how we've been treated. You *are* a chain with a motto you don't live up to. And *your* name, I see by your nameplate, is Bruce Valentine." My father turned to Ted. "Write that name down, son."

"Yes, *sir!*" said Ted enthusiastically, as if he'd just been inducted into the service of his country and was pleased with his first order. There was no pencil or paper around, but that was okay. It was the unbroken rhythm of this song-and-dance that counted.

My mother picked up the beat. "Also," she said, "the local police will want to investigate what's going on at that convention party. A drug bust is always a feather in the cap for a police department."

Bruce Valentine's eyes darted from one member of our family to another. The elf with the green ears who had checked this troublemaking family into the motel would probably be fired tomorrow. Bruce Valentine did not appear to know how to return money. His education was limited to credit cards.

"Well, folks," he said, smiling, "we want you to be satisfied." He thumbed through a large book on his desk. "We have a vacancy in the other wing. No conventioneers. And it's on the second floor. Nobody will be above you. It's a delightful room."

"Room?" said my father. "We need two adjoining rooms."

"We don't have two rooms, adjoining or separate. This is a very popular motel. The only other vacancy we have is for a suite of three bedrooms which also includes a small kitchen. But it's our highest-priced facility."

My mother drew herself up to her full height, which wasn't very high at all, but she fixed her eyes on Bruce Valentine as if she were far more formidable than her doll-like appearance in an outdated chenille bathrobe would suggest.

"You have a choice, Mr. Valentine," she said, "before I make mine to call the local police."

We all looked at her, astonished. My mother, the parent, the worrier, the settled schoolteacher, knew how to fight dirty. We were all proud of her.

Bruce Valentine didn't blink an eye. Pretending he didn't hear what my mother had just said, he announced, "The policy of this motel is to ensure the pleasure and comfort of all its guests. You may have the suite for the same price as the two rooms you are vacating. I'll mark the records. Here are the keys to the suite. After you have vacated your rooms, kindly turn in the keys to me."

Bruce Valentine handed my mother the keys to an entire suite. We went back to our rooms and quickly packed up. "Look under the beds. Look in the drawers. Don't leave anything on the closet shelves," my mother warned.

"Can I take the stationery to show my friends?" asked Heidi.

"Sure," said Ted.

Heidi also took a wrapped bar of soap.

We moved in ten minutes. Ted left the keys at the office. The suite was gorgeous. It was like a real apartment. Three bedrooms! My mother and father took one, Ted took one, and Heidi and I took the one at the farthest end of the suite.

I was too awake to try to sleep. I went into my parents' room. They were still unpacking. I sat on a bed. "This room is okay," I said.

"Yes, finally," said my mother.

"Tonight in the motel office I realized something. This is everybody's trip. I loved the way both of you stood up to that man in the office. And Ted and Heidi put in their two cents, too. I guess this *is* a family vacation, just like you said, and not just two parents and three unwilling victims."

I hugged my parents and left the room before they could say anything. It's easy to get teary and sentimental when you're tired, and it looked like they were going to let it all pour out.

I went to my bedroom, which was the last one in the string of three. Heidi was fast asleep. I climbed into my bed. Knowing that there was no one above me gave me a feeling of peace. It was more than a feeling. It *was* peace.

"Oh, honey!"

What? A disembodied voice. Could I have fallen asleep and dreamed about Neal? No. The voice was coming from the room next to mine. The head of my bed was next to the wall. The head of the bed in the next room must have been next to the wall. Apparently there were two people in the bed in the next room and they were madly in love. There was no convention in this wing of the motel, but the thin walls must be a feature throughout.

The bed in the next room squeaked and squeaked. It was embarrassing to think about what they, whoever they were, were doing in there. I think the girl's name was Sally. I felt like an eavesdropper. They stopped talking, but the bed kept squeaking, which, under the circumstances, was an eloquent sound.

I wondered what the rooms were like at Old Southwest. We probably would have gotten a good night's sleep. It would have been worth it to double back and find the place. I had tried to cut down on my father's fatigue, but it hadn't worked out any better.

In the morning we decided to pack up and leave. Our family was ready to move on and nobody felt like staying around this place. I noticed the backs of the loving couple next door as they were also leaving. The man was leaning into the trunk of his car. He was dressed in dark-blue shorts with a shiny light-blue stripe on the side, and a matching shirt. Very well dressed. "Sally" looked tacky. A girl doesn't usually wear a pink leather body suit early in the morning. I tried to ignore them. I knew too much about them. Suddenly I knew more. The man straightened up and turned around. It was Kip! Had I inadvertently attended Kip's party after all?

I looked at the room number of our suite. It was 210. Next door to Kip on the other side, another couple had come out. The man was dressed in a T-shirt and slacks. The woman was in her early-morning attire of green sequins. Then another couple came out. Kip started to joke with them.

Now I was dying to ask Ted what had happened with Kip. Ted had obviously chosen a card game with an elderly lady and a kid over whatever Kip had to offer. Although I didn't *know* what Kip had to offer, I had a pretty good idea. My little brother had chosen wisely. My little brother was growing up. So was I.

Dear Kristi,
In the middle of the night I met another new guy. His name was Valentine, but he wasn't as romantic as you might think. ♡ *Mia*

10

We had breakfast in a fast-food place. Ted and Heidi finished first and went over to the far corner of the room to play a video machine. My parents and I sat at the table drinking coffee. "Where to next?" I asked.

"Straight ahead," said my father, "until we find a place worth staying in for more than a night. Too bad we didn't go back and look for Old Southwest. We would have been better off than spending the night in that miserable noise factory."

"Much better off," I said. My mother looked at me. All of a sudden I found myself telling my parents how Neal and I had planned to meet.

"Why didn't you tell us?" said my father. "I certainly was willing to go back. Your mother and I were interested in seeing the place and the Guests were lovely people. It would have worked out."

My mother was cautious, but sympathetic. "To

turn back for a boy, I don't know. But he's clean-cut. Still, you don't know him very well. Then again, his demeanor is certainly respectable. I'm sorry, Mia, that you're so disappointed. But why didn't you tell us about this yesterday?"

"I couldn't tell you yesterday. Today we're more together or something."

"It's too late to go back now," said my father.

"But," said my mother, "it isn't too late to phone Neal and explain."

"Phone him? Mother, how?"

"Simple. The place has a telephone number, I'm sure. All you have to do is call and see if he's still registered."

"Then what do I say?" I couldn't believe I was asking my mother what to say to a boy.

"Just explain why you didn't show up. We're willing to pay for the call."

"Oh, thank you," I said, and I kissed her.

I collected dimes, nickels, and quarters from my parents. I went to the phone booth, which was outside. The weather felt hot and I felt hot thinking about what I was about to do. I didn't have any trouble getting through to Old Southwest. But getting through made me feel more nervous. I was one step closer to talking to Neal. The person who answered the phone at Old Southwest informed the operator that, yes, they did have a Guest family registered. There was a little confusion when the operator first asked for a guest named Guest, and there was some laughter, which loosened things up a bit for me. Now they were ringing the room.

Neal's mother answered. "Hi," I said. "This is Mia Fisher and I'm calling long-distance. Is Neal there, please?"

I hoped the words "long-distance" would get Mrs. Guest off the line in a hurry.

"Neal is right here. Just a moment, please."

"Hello."

"Neal, it's me, Mia."

"I don't believe it. Where are you?"

"I'm not anywhere near you. We missed our exit. It's a long story. But I wanted to call and explain."

"I've been waiting for you."

"I hoped you were. But in a way I hoped you weren't. I feel so terrible about not showing up."

"Look, maybe we can still meet. Where are you going next?"

"Who knows? My parents don't make reservations in advance, remember?"

"Okay, well, listen. I think we're staying here for one more night. Then we're moving on to that ranch. You've got the address. We'll be there a few nights. We stayed there for a week a couple of years ago, and I can personally recommend it. Horses, mountains, good food, swimming. A great time. Should I stay on the phone while you ask your folks?"

"No. I may have to do a sales job, and I'm short of change. Is the place on the way to Dallas?"

"I don't know where you are."

"Right. Well, I'm going to run out of money. I'll try to talk them into it. If I don't, write to me at my aunt and uncle's, okay?"

"I was going to anyway."

The operator was asking for more change. I was out.

"Are you involved with anyone at home?" Neal asked. "I never asked you."

"I've been going out with three guys, which means I don't really have a boyfriend. They're just dates." I had to be honest with him. "How about you?"

The operator cut us off. For another quarter or so I could have purchased vital information, but I was pretty sure that Neal didn't have a girlfriend. The way he acted, he didn't.

I went back to my parents' table. They were finished with their coffee and they were waiting for me. "He's not mad or anything," I said. "He was happy I called. And he has a great suggestion for us for a place to stay. He'll be there for a few nights starting tomorrow night. It's a guest ranch, and his family stayed there before. He really raved about it. Horses, mountains, good food, swimming. His mother is fussy about where they stay, too. Remember the motel where you met them? That was a decent place, wasn't it? But last night, when we just picked a place out of a hat, well, look what happened."

"You're suggesting we check in at this ranch," said my father. "And you'll meet Neal there. Is that it?"

"Not necessarily in that order," said my mother.

104

She was smiling. She wasn't so bad. After all, it was her idea to call Neal.

"Heidi and Ted would like it, too," I said. "Heidi likes horses, remember?"

"Only on television," said my mother.

"So, shall we make a reservation?" I asked.

"Reservation?" My mother's eyebrows went up. "I don't make reservations. First I see, then I decide."

"But what if they're full?"

"Can't help it. On this family vacation this is the way we travel."

"Okay. It's better than nothing. I still have hope."

"Hold on," said my father. "You're both standing at the gates of that ranch already. Who says we're going? We have to know where it is first, then we decide if we're willing to travel in that direction, then we find out exactly how to get there. No more missed exits. Mia, you have the name and address, I hope."

I pulled the torn half of the saleslip out of my pocketbook. I read the name and address of the guest ranch to my father.

"That's in a nice area," he said. "We have to think about that, too. If your mother doesn't like the ranch, we at least should be in a place with other attractions."

My father studied his map. He always seemed to be taking it out of his pocket and putting it back. It was too big and bulky for his pocket, but so was a security blanket, and this, I think, was his version of one. "Okay," he said finally. "If we were heading straight

105

for Dallas, this ranch would be about seventy-five miles out of the way. That's not bad, considering the side trips we figured we'd make anyway. We were allowing about a week in all to get to Dallas. We've been on the road three days. We could take in some sightseeing along the way today and arrive at the ranch sometime tomorrow, stay at the ranch two or three nights, and then push on to Dallas. The ranch is about a day's drive from Dallas."

"What are the chances of getting lost?" asked my mother.

"Minimal."

"Well, then, it's fine with me."

I nodded yes, of course.

My father got up and went over to Ted and Heidi. Then he came back. "Heidi says she's hungry and she can't make a decision without something to eat."

"She just had breakfast," said my mother. "Those video games give her a greater appetite than TV, and that was bad enough. Let's get out of here."

We dragged Ted and Heidi outside. We didn't physically drag them, but they looked as if they were moving under duress. They said a guest ranch sounded like fun, but they didn't have any boots. "We'll get you some," said my father.

"Is that a promise?" asked Heidi.

"No."

We spent most of the day sightseeing. We visited a museum, several restored historical homes, a broken-down fort, and a ghost town. I don't think any of these places were authentic. I think the fort was built up so it could be broken down. The museum seemed to be a home for trinkets, and the restored historical homes featured vendors of pecans and souvenir rocks. But the biggest adventure was finding a place to stay for the night. How can you judge whether or not a place has thin walls? Do you go around tapping?

"Let's just stay at a cheap place," said my mother. "If it's no good, at least we won't have overpaid."

"Do cheap places have TV sets?" asked Heidi. She was still tuned in to that.

"Probably," said my mother. "Now, are we all agreed on cheap for tonight?"

The three of us in the back raised hands.

We checked in at a place called THE DUMP, INC. A no-frills motel. It was one of those enterprises that brag about how cruddy-looking they are. Actually it was a chain of motels that was coming up in the world. Kristi had stayed in one once with her family and they liked it. My mother insisted on seeing the rooms before we checked in. They looked plain and kind of sincere in their plainness. "They'll do," she said.

They didn't have adjoining rooms. This time we three kids decided to sleep in the same room. Heidi and I took the bed. Ted had a cot. "Is it okay for a boy to sleep in our room?" asked Heidi.

"As long as the boy is Ted," I said.

"You won't peek when I get undressed, will you?" asked Heidi.

"Yeah, I'm so interested in what you look like," said Ted.

107

I was surprised my parents didn't mind not having adjoining rooms. Were they finally admitting we could take care of ourselves?

As it turned out, Heidi and I were happy to share a room with Ted. The first roach appeared about five minutes after we had unpacked. Ted raised his sneaker and, squish, no roach.

Heidi was hysterical. "If there's one, there's more. They come in families."

"I'll take care of them," said Ted. "They're nothing, just little bugs. No sweat."

Ted's sneaker became busy. "There, over there!" Heidi screamed.

"I see one!" I yelled.

Ted didn't know which way to turn first.

We were part of what seemed to be a classic sexist scenario. The big brave guy rescuing the two frightened girls. And that's exactly what it was. Ted wasn't afraid of roaches, and Heidi and I were. These crawling things with their obscene little legs and shiny little bodies made me quiver with terror. They had outlived dinosaurs.

"I'm moving," said Heidi.

I remembered the hassle at last night's motel. I couldn't believe we'd have to go through that all over again. "I'm going to Mom's and Dad's room and check the situation there," I said.

The room was four doors away. I knocked.

"Who is it?" my mother called.

"Me."

My mother unlocked the door. I walked in. I looked

108

around and especially down. I didn't see anything crawling.

"Mia, I don't want you walking around alone outside," said my mother.

"I'm not. I just came from my room to see how you like your room. What do you think of the accommodations?"

"They're cheap, they're clean—no frills, but no problems." My mother was smiling.

My father nodded. "At last, real value for our money. But how does Heidi feel about not having a TV set?"

"Uh, she hasn't noticed. We're kind of busy."

"Well, don't unpack everything. We're only here for one night," said my mother.

"So," I said, "you really like this place for sure?"

My mother looked at me suspiciously. "I shouldn't? I know it's not grand, but as your father says, it's good value. And the walls are thick. We can't hear a thing outside this room."

"Sleep at last," said my father. "No more cuckoo clocks, no more conventions, just sleep."

"Right," I said. "See you in the morning."

"Now be sure to lock and bolt your door, Mia," said my mother. "Can I depend upon you to do that?"

"Yes, Mom."

I kissed my parents good night. There are some deceptions that you put over on your parents that do not bring pangs of guilt. The roach deception fitted the bill. Whatever caused my parents' room to be roach-free and ours to be infested I didn't know. Maybe

109

someone had simply neglected to spray our room. I went back to it and bolted the door behind me. Ted, Heidi, and I and the roaches were safely bolted in for the night.

I gave my report. "They love their room they're tired, and they're looking forward to a good night's sleep. We can't make them get up and move again."

Heidi and Ted agreed. "I suggest shifts," said Ted. "I'll watch for the first two hours, then Mia, you take the next two, and then Heidi."

"I don't squish roaches," said Heidi. "Yuck!"

"Maybe they go to sleep when the light's out," I said.

"No, the opposite," said Ted. "That's when they get up. They like the dark. I'm surprised that these were out in the light."

"What if we keep the lights on," I suggested.

"Well, maybe," said Ted.

"I can't sleep with the lights on," said Heidi.

Heidi often falls asleep with the lights on. She just doesn't know it.

"More lights, fewer roaches," I said.

"Sold," said Heidi.

"Okay, you two go to bed," said Ted. "I'll have one sneaker ready here by my cot. I'll leave my other sneaker by your bed. You'll need it. Don't try to kill a roach with your sandals."

"We appreciate you, Ted," said Heidi. "Don't we, Mia?"

"Now and then," I said. But I gave Ted a small hug. When we got back home, I would put in a pitch for him to have his own car once he got his license. We couldn't afford it, and he certainly couldn't afford it, but it would be a united family goal. I really loved my brother and sister. We were having a good time together. Maybe it wasn't the kind of wonderful time you were supposed to have on a vacation. Actually it was a repulsive kind of wonderful time with the roaches. But it gave me a good feeling.

Ted fell asleep over his sneaker. I didn't find out until the next morning. He never mentioned whether he killed dozens of roaches or no roaches before he conked out. He didn't wake Heidi or me. We all slept through the night.

It was decided not to have a supermarket breakfast in our rooms the next morning. The motel fortunately had no coffee shop, so Ted, Heidi, and I didn't have to worry about eating on the premises at all. My father found an old white shingled diner a few miles down the road where we all stuffed ourselves on greasy doughnuts. Then we headed straight for the ranch. The ranch and Neal.

//

Why didn't anyone tell me that ranches attract beautiful girls? At least the Calle Conquistador Guest Ranch did. That's the first thing I noticed when we drove up. All those beautiful girls with long wavy hair, strutting around, riding around, swarming around in their tight jeans and plaid shirts. Ted noticed, too. "Nice place," he said, and he gave a little whistle.

"Horses!" said Heidi. "Just like on the reruns of *Bonanza*."

To me the ranch had been a place, *the* place for my reunion with Neal. I had pictured something private and corny, like our standing next to a split-rail fence in the sunset. I wanted it to be romantic. As for other people, I figured there would be some my parents' age and some weathered-looking ranch hands and a grizzly-looking cook. I did not expect the ranch to resemble an outdoor beauty pageant.

We once went to Las Vegas and there were all these showgirls dressed in short fringed skirts and boots and cowboy hats. They were doing this kind of sexy dance with a cowgirl theme. Someone in the audience snickered, if only cowgirls really looked like that. At least at this ranch they do. Of course I don't know a cowgirl from a guest, but the label doesn't matter. The girls at this ranch were unfortunately outstanding. I had a one-minute fantasy in which these girls did the commercial they were brought here to do, then scrambled aboard a pickup truck and were driven down a dusty road, out of sight forever.

We checked in at the office. My eyes were everywhere looking for Neal. I felt too self-conscious to ask if his family had checked in yet. I was also too uptight about our situation. We had no reservations. Was there a vacancy or would we be turned away? There were vacancies. My luck hadn't completely run out. In fact, we had a choice of three different-sized "ranch houses" as they were called. We took the middle size.

Our ranch house was about half a mile from the office. It had two bedrooms, a stone fireplace, a big braided rug, rustic furniture, and bunklike beds with woolen blankets. The house smelled of wood. My parents were delighted with it.

As we unpacked in our new and last place before our final spurt to Dallas, I thought it was all worth it. This was where Neal and I *planned* to meet. Everything was arranged. I wouldn't have to hang out by a pool and wonder if I'd meet anyone. I wouldn't have to visit my mother's friend. I probably wouldn't have to battle roaches or put up with noisy neighbors. We had our own little ranch house. This was perfection. It was everything a vacation was supposed to be according to Kristi. It was romance, fun, and adventure. Almost. I hadn't seen Neal yet.

We got ready for lunch. That was another plus about this place. We had to eat in their dining room. We were paying for it. It was part of the deal. No more supermarket breakfasts or greasy joints. The dining room was big and sunny, with long bare wooden tables and plain straight-backed chairs. There were various pictures and hangings on the walls, about evenly divided among a horse theme, a cow theme, and a lonely-cowboy theme. The waiters and waitresses were mostly young and wore tan shirts, jeans, and boots.

The dining room was about half-full. The five of us sat down at the end of one of the long empty tables. My father sat at the very end, then my mother, Heidi, Ted, and me. We faced air. My parents were eager for some adult company. In particular they were looking for Neal's parents. My mother knew I was watching for Neal, but she didn't say anything.

Ted and Heidi kept quiet about Neal, too. I hadn't confided in them, but somehow they got the vibes and they knew what was going on. My mother had at one point declared that we were going to meet the "Guest family" here. "Big guests and little guest," Ted had kidded.

We had stew for lunch. It was ordinary, but it was

served with home-baked rolls that Ted, Heidi, and I devoured. We had gelatin with oatmeal cookies for dessert. This seemed to be the kind of place where it was against the law to serve anything sophisticated.

I was eating my gelatin when *they* walked in. "They" were the Guests *and* a spectacular-looking girl. Too spectacular for me. And she looked older. Too old for Neal. I stared at them and then I stared down at my gelatin. It was lemon gelatin. Suddenly it looked like a sickly sparkling arrangement of yellow glass. This is the stuff they feed patients in hospitals who are too ill to eat anything else. It was too potent for me to handle. Something terrible and dead settled into my stomach. There was certainly no room for lemon gelatin.

"Hey, there are the Guests," said Ted. "And who's the great-lookin' chick with them? She's a . . ."

Ted looked at me. He was sorry he had said anything. He was actually becoming sensitive.

"It's okay, Ted," I said. "I appreciate your stopping in midsentence. It's nice to know one thoughtful guy, even if he is my kid brother."

"I bet she's his sister," said Heidi. "Things like this always happen on *Lovestream*."

"What's *Lovestream*?" asked Ted.

"A television program, of course," said Heidi. "Every week lovers get mad and they break up through mistakes and misunderstandings, and everything comes out okay in the end. It only takes an hour." Heidi leaned in front of Ted so she could confide in me. "This girl that Neal's with could really be

115

his sister or his cousin or his riding instructor. Yuh, that works out logically. She's his riding instructor. Neal is nice. He wouldn't be mean."

"She looks too unathletic to be a riding instructor. What if she's his girlfriend?"

"That doesn't happen on *Lovestream* unless she's meant to be his girlfriend. You can see that this girl wasn't meant to be Neal's girlfriend."

"How can you watch that junk?" asked Ted.

My mother and Mrs. Guest exchanged waves. The Guests and the girl came up to our table. My father stood up and shook hands with Mr. Guest. Before I could even imagine what to do, Neal gave me a big hi. Then they all sat down across from us. Mrs. Guest took the seat opposite my father and immediately started to talk to him. Mr. Guest sat opposite my mother. Neal and the girl sat down last. I don't know how it happened but Neal landed opposite Heidi, and the girl sat down beside him opposite Ted as if she were part of the Guest family.

"Hi. I'm Beth Ann Wagner."

That was it. No reason for her to be with them. No mention that she was a relative, a riding instructor, anything.

"What do you do?" asked Heidi.

In their own way, Heidi and Ted were rallying around me. When I was at home, why hadn't I appreciated them? Because I had my own friends. Now they were my allies. Remember that, Mia, when you get home.

Beth Ann seemed puzzled by Heidi's question. Then

I guess she decided she hadn't heard right. Heidi must have said how do you do. Beth Ann replied with a smile.

Ted said, "What brings you here?"

"I'm on vacation," said Beth Ann. "I'm making a great time for myself."

So much for the riding instructor. I wondered, Was she on vacation with *Neal*? Where had she been earlier? Did Neal just pick her up? Had he planned to meet *both* of us here? Was Neal that most loathsome of all guys, a girl collector? Come here, girl, and become another notch on my belt. And what better place than at a ranch.

Was Neal's mother thrilled that Neal had found Beth Ann? I bet his mother got my postcard and didn't give it to him. Every time she saw a container of ketchup she knew there were more suitable girls in the world for her son than me. I didn't care what his mother or father thought, but somehow it hurt to be looked down upon, to be thought unsuitable while they enthroned another girl. Princess Beth Ann had very small, delicate features, the kind that look good from every angle, the kind that never fail you.

Ted was sizing her up. He had stopped eating and was devoting himself to this project. What did he look like to her? Of course I knew what he looked like because I saw him all the time. But I wondered how he would seem to a new girl. My girlfriends back home thought he was cute. There was something about the expression around his mouth. They said it was a rock star's mouth. It was, in fact, an orthodontist's mouth. My parents had spent a fortune getting his teeth straightened. His eyes were dark, burning brown. Under certain conditions, conditions never quite clear to me, my brother Ted could be considered a sex object. I let him do all the talking to Beth Ann. I was still sitting across from air. I thought she was too much for Neal, but what did it matter what I thought. She was certainly too much for Ted, but she definitely knew how to listen when a boy was talking.

Maybe I was overthinking. Maybe Beth Ann was just a girl the Guests had met outside the dining room. Five minutes ago. People on vacation strike up conversations with strangers. I should know.

"Boy, am I ever sore!" Beth Ann announced as she ate a roll.

"Sore?" Ted was interested.

"From square dancing. It's not as easy as it looks. When Neal and I went square dancing last night I didn't know what I was getting into."

Neal and Beth Ann together dancing! So much for the just-met theory. I looked over at Neal. He seemed about to say something. But Beth Ann went on. "I'm going to train before I do it again."

"How do you go into training for square dancing?" asked Heidi.

"There must be a way," Beth Ann said.

"Maybe you should just sit and watch," said Heidi.

Before Beth Ann could answer, Heidi started to talk to Neal across the table. But she got drowned out by the conversation going on between my parents and

Neal's parents. I could hear them from my end of the table. Neal's father was buzzing away with tales of Old Southwest, including the news that it was vastly overrated. "Just a tourist trap. They were hawking cowboy hats on every other corner. We checked out of there and came here yesterday. We had planned to stay longer, but we cleared out before they could sell us a plastic cactus."

This was interesting. The Guests had checked in yesterday. When yesterday? Had Neal spent most of the afternoon with Beth Ann? In addition to the evening?

Mr. Guest didn't say anything else because Mrs. Guest took over. She seemed annoyed by her husband's frankness. She leaned across the table toward my father. "Tell us about *your* vacation."

My father related our experiences at the noisy motel. Mrs. Guest started to laugh. "Can't you just see Alfie in the same situation? He would have threatened to call the newspapers, the television stations . . ."

My mother looked puzzled. "Why would the media be interested?"

"You don't know Alfie," said Mrs. Guest. "He'd *make* them interested. Don't you think so, Hugh?"

I guess my mother couldn't help disliking Alfie Mink. She said quietly, "Yes, he'd do that."

The Guests were served lunch while my family sat and kept them company. They were served apple pie for dessert. I guess the lemon gelatin was so popular it got used up.

"I love apple pie," exclaimed Beth Ann.

She would, I thought. And she probably won't gain an ounce.

"It's my favorite," Ted said. He didn't have to humble himself that way. Ted thought apple pie was dumb. It had a bad rep. It used to be a food, but now it was a salute to morality.

After the meal Mrs. Guest said, "We're all going horseback riding." Then she looked across the table at my father. "Do you ride, Hugh?"

"Ever since I was a kid at camp."

"Then do come with us."

"I don't know . . ."

"Go, dear," said my mother. "We *are* at a ranch."

Suddenly Mrs. Guest realized she hadn't invited the rest of our family. "You're all invited," she said, and without waiting to find out whether any of us were accepting, she stood up.

Everyone stood up. "We're going to change into our riding clothes," said Mrs. Guest. "We'll meet you at the stables in half an hour, Hugh. See you later, Gwen."

Neal came over to me. It was the first attention he showed me since he'd seen me again. "Want to go riding, Mia?"

I looked at Neal's eyes. Were they really as gentle as I first thought? What did he think of me? What did he really think of Beth Ann? I couldn't squelch my pride.

"No, thanks," I said, trying to sound calm.

"But we . . ."

"No, thanks. I have other plans."

Square dancing with Beth Ann. Riding with Beth Ann and me. I was not going to be one of his girls.

"I'll see you later then," he said, and he walked away. Was he mad? I stood there and watched him. I felt terrible.

Dear Kristi,
    It isn't looking nearly as good as I
thought.
                              Sick of love,
                              Mia

12

My father left to meet his horse. My mother and Heidi went for a stroll around the grounds. Ted said he was going exploring, whatever that meant. I went to the ranch gift shop to pick out a gift to send to Kristi.

I chose a fringed scarf with a picture of a horse on it for Kristi. It was the thought that counts. The gift shop did the mailing if you paid the postage.

I thought about Kristi. What would she have done in my situation? Would she be in a gift shop picking out presents while an apple-pie princess rode off into the sunset with her guy? Not in a million years. Kristi would fight for what she wants. I wanted Neal. I knew how to fight, didn't I? Not for a guy I didn't. But I could learn. I had to think about this. I wasn't going to give up.

I walked slowly back to the ranch house. I saw my father and Mrs. Guest just outside. She gave me a long look. Was she glad I wasn't with Neal? Where was Neal anyway? Was he still with Beth Ann?

"Hester's here to borrow our coffeepot," my father explained. "I'll be right back," he said, and he went inside the house. A moment later he was back with our aluminum coffeepot. He handed it to Hester.

"I so appreciate this, Hugh," she said. "I'll return it later."

"No rush."

"Well, I'll see you and Gwen at dinner. Now don't forget about the movie."

Hester walked off, holding our coffeepot as if it were a trophy.

"She's crazy about coffee," my father said. "And they didn't bring a pot with them. We won't miss this."

"Did you offer it or did she ask you for it?"

"She asked to borrow it after I happened to mention we had it."

"You should have asked Mom first. I think she's annoyed with Hester and all of her stories about Alfie Mink."

"Those were great times, Mia, when I knew Alfie. Recalling them makes me feel young all over again. Don't knock it."

"Dad, I think you have vacation fever," I said.

"What's that?"

"Something I used to have."

My mother and Heidi came back while my father and I were still standing in the doorway. I wondered if my mother caught sight of Hester triumphantly carrying off our coffeepot.

"Have a good walk?" I asked.

"Terrific," my mother said. Her face was flushed. "How was your ride, Hugh?"

"I'm a little sore, but I'll recover."

Just then Ted came along. "This place goes on and on and on," he said. "It's tremendous."

We all went into the house. Heidi turned on the television set. "This is just like home," she said. "Our own house and television. This is neat."

"No, it's not," Ted said, laughing.

We were keeping the sleeping arrangements we had at The Dump, Inc. My parents in one bedroom; Heidi, Ted, and me in the other. I was glad my parents had some privacy. I wondered when my mother would have a yen for a cup of her own plugged-in instant coffee.

She walked into the bedrooms. "We have piles of dirty laundry just like at home," she said. "Who wants to do it?"

"I will," said Ted.

I was shocked until my mother said, "There's a busy laundry room on the premises. We walked by it."

Busy. That must mean there were girls there. Otherwise why would Ted volunteer? He was always alert to where the action was. I could take a few lessons from him. Where, for example, was Neal right now?

"I'm going for a walk," I said.

"All right," said my mother. "But be back before dark. Be back before dinner. Remember there are dining-room hours here. We have to eat when they want us to eat."

"I'll remember." I stepped outside. The weather was hot and dry. I started to walk. I walked by the pool and the stables and even the laundry room. Neal was nowhere. I was also looking for Beth Ann. If I saw her without Neal, that would be fine with me.

By the time I got back, everyone was getting ready for dinner. My father was busy unpinning a new shirt and removing the tissue paper. "Why, Hugh, you're actually getting into a new shirt. I can't believe it," said my mother.

"Well, an old shirt has to be new first. I can't get around that." He laughed.

Was he trying to look his best for the Guests?

Suddenly I was very very sorry we had ever met the Guest family.

I couldn't imagine what dinner would be like. We were supposed to be eating with the Guests, of course. Afterward my parents were going into town with Mr. and Mrs. Guest to see a movie. This wonderful plan had been initiated by Hester Guest, who, I was sure by now, wanted something from my father. I wasn't sure what. My mother was worried about what Ted, Heidi, and I would be doing. I was also worried about what I would be doing. Where was Neal? He said he'd see me later. It already was later. But was it too late?

We had the same cast of characters for dinner that we had for lunch, meaning Beth Ann Wagner was there along with Neal and his parents. We sat exactly where we had sat at lunch, which reminded me of a classroom where you have assigned seats.

Beth Ann was full of conversation. Neal's mother looked happy. She was really dressed up in a blue-green dress that looked like it should have been on a teenage model, matching earrings, and a kind of long, flowing hairdo. She had a dozen slender bracelets on one arm. In comparison, my mother looked like a doll in a white ruffled dress. She always wore her hair the same. It was short and she didn't have much to work with. My mother was doing more listening than talking.

It didn't matter what Beth Ann was wearing. Everything worked with her face. By the time dessert, one lone brownie on a lacy little napkin, arrived, I was tired of looking at her face and Neal's face and everybody's face. I got up from the table and excused myself.

I had no idea where I was going. Everyone probably thought I was headed for the ladies' room. I went outside. There were benches all around and I sat down on one of them. I thought about the entire vacation. It had been a revelation. I was surprised to see how some adults behaved. Hester Guest, Lizette Trumbull . . . what an education. As for Neal, maybe it had been a dumb arrangement to meet him here. That Beth Ann . . . so empty! Couldn't Neal see that? She *was* beautiful. Guys are flattered when a beautiful girl looks their way. But he deserved better than empty. He deserved me. But how could I fight for him? I needed an opportunity.

No one at home could ever know about this.

The best part of the vacation had been being with the family. Now I knew what space really means. When you're literally short of it, something happens to your relationships. If you're lucky, they grow. Even with a cramped car and strange motel rooms, it felt good to be with people who loved me and cared about one another.

How long could I sit here? I was waiting for something to happen. Was this my idea of fighting for Neal? I guess I thought that Neal was supposed to run out after me and tell me how much he loved me. That's the way it was supposed to happen. The girl runs away, the guy goes after her. What was causing the delay?

The delay was caused by Neal's not having left his chair. He had no intention of going after me. Of course, if he thought I was headed for the ladies' room, it was understandable. But he could have checked up on my absence. I saw that Neal hadn't left his seat when I returned to the dining room. I had to go back. I couldn't wreck everybody's evening by disappearing. My lonesome brownie was still waiting for me.

When dinner was over, we all got up and kind of grouped together as if someone were about to take our picture. Then my parents and Neal's parents took off for the movies. That left five of us juvenile types adrift for the evening. Ted grabbed Beth Ann's arm and they walked off together. It was done swiftly, as if they had rehearsed and were able to do it without any hesitation or flaws in execution. I was dumbfounded. Had he spent time with her at the laundry room? Had they planned this while I was warming the bench outside?

Neal seemed surprised, too. Well, really, what did he expect? Beth Ann was out for a good time, and Ted probably knew it. Neal should have known it earlier. Maybe he didn't even know it now. Beth Ann was another Kip. Vacation Fast Action. It was obvious to *me*. Why wasn't it to Neal?

He looked at me. "Mia, I'm so glad you're here."

"Really?"

Heidi was beside me. She said "Really?" too.

"What about Beth Ann?" I asked.

"She's fun."

"She seems flighty," I said. "Actually, she's an airhead. Didn't you notice?"

Was I fighting for Neal or with him? I was so angry I couldn't tell the difference.

I went on. "You could have excused yourself from going riding with her and your mother and spent time with me instead."

Neal was silent.

"Maybe your mother tells you what to do and who to like. She doesn't like me. What's her thing, anyway? Borrowing coffeepots?"

"If we're discussing my mother, she's a complex person. But, Mia, I *did* ask you to go riding with us.

128

There were so many people around, it was hard to break away. You didn't want to be with me."

"I think it's *you*, Neal, who hasn't figured out what you want yet." Suddenly I was calm. "You really haven't," I said almost in a whisper.

I walked away and pulled Heidi with me.

Dear Kristi,
  You wouldn't want to know what happened.
                            Distraught Mia

13

A temper is a good thing and a bad thing. Getting mad can be a real high. The problem is that it usually comes just before a real low. Maybe I was unfair to Neal. But if Ted hadn't yanked Beth Ann out of the picture, what would Neal have done? Would he have done anything? It was inconceivable that he just would have gone along without *being* with me. This was our reunion place. I got angry because I wasn't sure about anything. It's fine to be an accepting angel, but what if it means you're an accepting idiot?

"Where did you learn to get mad like that?" asked Heidi. We were walking around the grounds.

"I guess I don't want to talk about any of this, Heidi," I said.

"Can I go swimming?"

"Only if there's somebody else in the pool. You can't go in alone. Those are orders."

"Okay."

The pool was deserted. We took off our shoes, sat down, and dangled our feet in the shallow end. "This is a dumb way to spend the night," said Heidi. "I want to go swimming and you want to be with him."

We sat there forlornly, like two rejects from civilization, taking solace in the eerily lighted green water. We kicked our feet back and forth.

"Let's go home and watch TV," I said.

"You must feel terrible," said Heidi.

"You get to pick the programs," I answered.

We watched TV until Ted got home. Then we turned off the set. We wanted to hear about his evening with Beth Ann. We sat there, eagerly waiting to invade his privacy. "It was a good night," he said. That was all he had to offer.

"Details, details," said Heidi.

"None of your business," said Ted. Crudely but well put.

My parents were next to arrive. They came in about an hour after Ted. They were willing to talk about their evening. "The movie was a riot," said my mother. "Well acted, well directed. I'm afraid Hester Guest didn't like it, though. I can't understand that. Didn't she laugh at all, Hugh? She was sitting beside you."

My father shrugged.

"Did you go anyplace after the movie?" Heidi asked.

"Just out to eat in a coffee shop. There's not much to do in town," my father said.

"Eat," said Heidi. "You're so lucky. I want to eat.

Why doesn't this house have a kitchen if it's called a house?"

"Because there's a main dining room and that's where we're supposed to eat, that's what we're paying for," said my mother. "But I knew you'd complain if we went out to eat and didn't bring back anything for you."

"You brought me a sundae? A taco? What did you bring?"

"I didn't bring a sundae or a taco or anything like that. It would be messy. I stopped in a convenience store and bought you something sweet. Hot chocolate. I bought more than enough for all of you."

My mother reached into her pocketbook and took out a small tin of hot-chocolate instant mix.

"I want something hot with a marshmallow floating in it," said Heidi. "What good is that old tin?"

"I'll heat up some water and we'll have hot chocolate."

"In Styrofoam cups?"

"I should have brought mugs on this trip. I can't think of everything. But this will be fun. I bought some cookies, too."

"Cookies? Okay, hot chocolate and cookies," said Heidi as if she had anything else to choose from. Heidi, the eleven-year-old glutton.

"How about you two?" asked my mother.

Ted yawned. "No, thanks."

I wasn't particularly hungry or thirsty, but my mother was pleased with herself for bringing home

132

this little treat and I didn't want to turn her down. "Okay," I said.

"I'll just get the coffeepot and heat up the water," she said.

The coffeepot! My mother is a coffee lover and I had already pictured her looking for our absent pot when the urge for a cup of instant hit her. Hot chocolate, on the other hand, had never entered my mind.

"We don't have it," said my father. He had probably stood by while my mother purchased the tin of hot chocolate, not connecting it to the chain of events that would inevitably follow.

"I lent it to Hester," he went on. "I had been telling her how useful our coffeepot has been while we were traveling. She thought that was a clever idea, and she wished she had thought of it. It seems she drinks about ten cups of coffee a day. She says it's an addiction. She hated to ask to borrow our pot, but . . ."

"What did she do for coffee before she met us?" Heidi asked.

"Good question," said my mother. "I'm beginning to feel annoyed with Hester. In fact, I *am* annoyed with Hester. I'm going over there and get my coffeepot back."

I remembered my mother's confrontation with Bruce Valentine, and I figured this had to be a thousand times better.

My father said, "No, I'll get it. I'm the one who lent it to her."

"Are you trying to avoid trouble?"

133

"Well, I'll just go and get it back—politely, of course—and then I think you and I should scout around for some other friends while we're here."

"Can I get the coffeepot back?" I asked.

"What is this, a coffeepot retrieving contest?" Ted asked.

I couldn't explain to them that I wanted to see Neal. I wouldn't be able to sleep if I didn't try to make up. "I'll get it," I repeated. "Just tell me where they're staying."

"But you can't walk out there alone at night," said my mother.

We were back to that.

"Besides, the family may have gone to bed. Did you spend the evening with Neal? I forgot to ask. Did you have a good time?"

"No, I didn't spend the evening with Neal. Heidi and I watched some thrilling TV programs."

"Oh, dear. What went wrong?"

Ted butted in. "I'll go with Mia. Is that okay? The two of us. I've had some karate lessons. On the way back, if necessary, we can use the coffeepot as a weapon."

"Ted, you're making fun of me." My mother was partially amused.

"Let them go," said my father. "It's less sticky."

"I'm eating cookies while I wait for the hot chocolate," said Heidi.

My mother kind of threw up her hands. "Whatever," she said.

134

"Let's get out of here," Ted said to me, and he half-pushed me out the door.

"I forgot to ask where they're staying." I turned around to go back.

"I know where. They mentioned it at dinner tonight."

"I had a fight with Neal after dinner. I started it."

"So end it. Go get the coffeepot and make up. I'll wait for you. I'll show you where their place is and then I'll wait for you in the distance."

"I'm not sure."

"Okay. It's up to you. I knew you wanted to get this coffeepot, and it's a great night for a walk. So I offered to go. But that's it. I can start your motor, but I can't move your chassis."

"I thought you gave up that language."

"I will never give up that language."

I shrugged and didn't answer. The sky was filled with stars and there was more poetry in the night than in our conversation. It was a night for silent walks, for wrapping the beauty of nature around us. Nature was arrogant. It was so much bigger than my problems. It dwarfed them without trying.

"Let's go home," I said. "Let's not spoil the walk. Why are we taking this walk anyway? To get an aluminum coffeepot?"

"That's the whole idea of it," said Ted. "And we're not going home without it."

I was so busy talking I didn't notice that someone was coming toward us. Suddenly Neal was standing

135

in front of us! He was holding something. The coffeepot.

Ted immediately turned and fled. I got the idea that he wanted Neal and me to be alone. He was kind of sweet.

"I was just coming to get that pot," I said to Neal.

"And I was just bringing it to you," he answered.

We stood silently facing each other. Then Neal said, "I was also coming to apologize. You were right about Beth Ann. But that's not important. You were right about me. I was flattered by Beth Ann's attention. She's just a passing thing. You're not. You never could be."

"I shouldn't have blown up the way I did. And I had no right to speak against your mother," I said.

"My mother . . ." Neal hesitated. "My mother's looking for the kind of attention she shouldn't be looking for. I'm heading off to college and the world, and she's afraid of getting old and of losing me. She's trying to find her youth again. She's jealous of you. You're so young and . . ."

"Foolish," I said. We both laughed.

"Is she after my father?" I had to ask.

"No, of course not, she's only trying to feel young. She's not so bad, but you really, really have to understand her, and that takes time and patience and maybe it takes being her blood relative. Why are we talking about my mother when we can talk about us?"

I knew why. I wasn't quite ready to accept *us*. I wanted to, but I couldn't.

"Neal, I have to think about what you said, about you, about us, okay?"

He seemed hurt. He didn't answer.

"Too much has happened today. I'm confused," I said.

"All right. I'll walk you home. We have to make sure that the coffeepot arrives safely." He laughed and we both felt better. We walked to my house.

Actually, I didn't really want to think about us. I wanted to reach up and give him a kiss, but I was afraid to. I needed the night to think.

At my door he said good night and walked away. I hoped I hadn't lost him.

Dear Kristi,
I'm so confused I think I should write you a letter.
Your friend,
Mia

14

The next morning my parents went off to play tennis, Heidi went off to the swimming pool, and Ted simply went off. I was the only one without a destination. I was too tired to think about it. I hadn't slept at all. At least I hadn't been aware of sleeping. They say that you sleep even when you think you don't.

I had an hour to go before the dining room closed for breakfast. I felt shaky about going into the dining room by myself. The rest of the family had already eaten, after trying unsuccessfully to revive me enough to go with them.

The sun was shining into the room. It glinted off the tin of hot-chocolate mix that was on the dresser. The modest tin of hot chocolate, promising sweet, velvety sensations and innocuous delights. Ha! I got up and checked to see if the lid was on. I saw an ant crawling up the side of the tin. I hate ants, but they're not as disgusting as roaches. I watched it. The minute it got to the top, I would kill it. Suddenly it flew off. A flying ant? Whatever it was, it was gone.

I showered and got dressed. Every time I got dressed I paid the price all over again for packing ratty-looking clothes. Aside from my swimsuit, that's all Neal had ever seen me in. The gift shop stocked Western-style clothes, but the prices were outrageous. When I got to Dallas, I could buy something. But it would be too late.

I brushed my hair. I was all ready for breakfast. Paint-stained shorts, a limp shirt, a limp brain. I was trying to remember what Neal had said last night. He wanted me back. I didn't dream it, did I? But did I wreck everything?

I glanced around the room. I was ready to leave. The ant had returned to the tin. Good. That would delay me for another minute or so while I got a tissue or something I could use to kill it. It was exciting to have a real project to launch my day. Something to get my blood moving. Welcome to the land of the nerds.

The ant flew off just as I heard a knock on the door. It was probably Heidi or Ted. They had gone off without keys. There weren't enough to go around.

I opened the door. Standing there was Neal.

"Good morning," he said.

"Good morning."

"Had breakfast?"

"No."

"Neither have I."

I think it was an invitation to have breakfast with

him. I stepped out, made sure the door was locked, and put the key in my pocket. I hoped Ted and Heidi wouldn't come back expecting to get in. My parents had the other key. We started to walk. And we talked. About the *weather*. Safe topic. So were horses and cacti. Through a trail of safe topics we made our way to the dining room.

We sat down at the end of a long table that we had to ourselves. We were served quickly. I think they wanted to get rid of us. Breakfast-serving hours were almost over.

I drank half of my orange juice. Then I said, "It's so strange about vacations. The people you meet, the way you meet them, the relationships, the lack of relationships. It's hard to trust someone you meet on a vacation. You know they'll be gone tomorrow or the next day, and there's a feeling that . . ."

Neal interrupted me. "I know. I have a confession to make. That's the way I felt about *you*. I didn't think you'd actually meet me here. You didn't make it to Old Southwest. Not that it was your fault. That's just the way it is on vacations. Why don't we respect vacation relationships? Why do we think that when we get back home we'll forget each other, that we're just temporary? Permanent to the people we've known a long time, but temporary to each other. It doesn't *have* to be that way, Mia. I won't let it be that way. I really like you."

Was I going to get a kiss over orange juice? I wasn't. I was going to get a dirty look from our waitress, who wanted to kick us out of the dining room.

We attacked our breakfasts. Good, honest Western breakfasts of eggs mixed with some kind of meat and beans. We laughed at each other's bad manners as we quickly gobbled everything up. We guzzled coffee. Fortunately it was warm to cool. It was the most wonderful of all breakfasts. Neal had summed it up: it doesn't *have* to be temporary.

Suddenly Heidi appeared in the dining room. She was dripping wet. One of the waitresses tried to stop her. "I'm locked out," she yelled to me. "You locked me out and I'm all wet."

Neal and I got up and left to the silent cheers of the waitress. The three of us walked back to the ranch house where Ted was sitting and waiting. "You locked him out, too," said Heidi. "From now on, I get the key. My snack is inside there, did you know that? You just ate, but it's been at least two hours for me."

I unlocked the door. Ted and Heidi walked inside, inside the little ranch house that would be our home away from home for another day or two. Then we would be off to Dallas and our aunt and uncle. We would stay there a week and then start the trip back. The trip back. I couldn't imagine what it would be like.

In the distance I saw my parents walking toward the house. They were with another couple. They had made new friends. Temporary or otherwise.

I threw the key inside to Ted and Heidi. "Catch," I said. Neal and I started to walk away.

"Where are you two going?" asked Heidi.

141

"Someplace special," I said. "We're on vacation, aren't we?"

Heidi yelled a moment later. No doubt she had inspected her newest off-hours food supply, the hot-chocolate tin, and found the ant in residence.

Ted, her big brother, would take care of it.

There was another shriek.

"Fifty cents? What do you mean fifty cents? You used to do it for free."

Neal and I kept walking.

I did not, could not, would not, think about the hundreds and hundreds and hundreds of backseat miles in my future.

Neal and I headed toward the woods. We sat down under a tree. I knew he was going to kiss me, just as he had that other time we sat under the tree at the motel. But this time I didn't have to worry about not seeing him again. I knew I'd see him, even when the vacation was over. We'd work it out.

My vacation fever was back! I was sure Neal had it, too. I had a confirmed case. I hope it rages forever and they never find a cure.